The Chatters Web

Peter J Morley

Copyright © 2025

Dedication

This novel is dedicated to those who write,

Beneath a burning candle, well into the night,

Who rise before dawn with minds alert

A new line, a new thought, a new word to insert.

Peter J Morley 13/3/2025

If you could take your first breath again

And know what you would learn

Would you set yourself upon the path

From which you would not turn.

Peter J Morley

13/3/2025

Acknowledgment

To those who journeyed with me in the writing of this novel I acknowledge their interest and extend my thanks

Writing a book is never an easy task, but the help that I received from family and friends was honestly offered and gladly accepted.

My 3 boys were happy to receive an initial copy of the manuscript!

Thank you to Anne de Carteret who planted the seed for the story.

Book Club members were keen to help and I thank Kim Wilks and Dorothy O'Brien for their contribution.

Thank you to friends Ishbel Taylor in Australia, Malcolm and Sue Morton in the UK, Mark Forbes in Cambodia, My Rotary friend Mike Spice in Australia et al.

Contents

The Chatter's Web.

Jean's phone rang, and the recorded message began ……, 'Hi, this is Jean. Sorry, I can't take the call at the moment. Just leave a message.'

'Jean, it's Lisbeth Hurley. How are you? All is well, I hope. Look, just a quick message. This is about Mia's death, of course. What else do I have in my life? I need to catch up with you soon. I may have a new client for you. I'm not really sure if you will want to meet him, but I'll get back to you…. He may be a lead to Mia's death or may at least know something that is useful. Keep your diary open. Talk soon. Bye.'

It was always the same for Jean. Her work contacts and friends know what she does, but whenever she was asked by others what she did for work, and she answered with a simple, 'I'm a Chatter,'……she would see the next question inevitably flick across their face, their brow would furrow, and they would ask,

'What the heck is a Chatter?'

Well, I'm happy to explain, she would say, as I have explained many times, but anyway, I am a paid 'Chatter.'

Although sometimes my relationships can go well and sometimes not so well. I do, sometimes, become caught up in their life.

It's pretty obvious really. You see, my job or my role in my client's lives is that of a Chatter. That's what I do. I'm simply paid to chat with people. My clients are elderly, retired, and nearly always on their own. There's no doubt that some of them have had unhappy and sometimes strained lives. Let's get to that later when I tell you their stories.

So, nine out of ten, or 90% of those who may prefer another way of looking at it, have nobody to talk to them. Sometimes, their only contact with another human is when they go shopping or wander through the markets looking like some lost soul on a mission.

But these days, even in the supermarket, they can't talk to the checkout lady because, quite often, they are directed through the self-serve lanes. If they don't take that option, then they have to wait in some endless queue whilst some poor old shopper empties their trolley onto the moving counter.

So what they do is ask for help whilst they are tramping up and down the shopping aisles, making an opportunity to talk to someone. Sometimes, it may be a staff member or a nice-looking man who can reach for a tin of something. How sad.

So you see, I'm the person who they can sit with and 'Chat.' I'm their secret confessional. I listen, and I help. I'm trusted…… but sometimes, I do end up becoming caught up in their lives. Especially when they don't know that their life intersects with another of my clients, hence the web that is woven.

I've always been a chatterbox. Even at school, I would get into trouble because I would chat too much in class. I never let a moment go by without chatting.

So when I call at my client's home on their selected day, they are usually really looking forward to their time 'chatting' with me. I am always surprised at how much they like to tell me how much they open up about their past, especially when I prompt them.

What I like to do is to help my clients reflect on their lives or reflect on life in general. I certainly like to do that. I ask things like, what dreams did you have that are unfulfilled, or do you have any secret memories? Those questions can open up many thoughts, which is what I want.

Settings

Most times I sit inside their house in their lounge room. That's interesting for me because I can understand them and get a better idea of their personality based on the items on their shelf or bookcase. Or any pictures hanging on the wall.

They'll make a cuppa and share a biscuit or two. However, a glass of wine goes down well. Come the summer we may sit outside on the veranda or balcony to get some sun and fresh air. I listen to their views on the government, or I hear about their past, their family, or the husband who has died, although I do have some clients who have divorced.

Sometimes, they tell me very personal stories. So …. I sit and Chat.

Purpose

Why do I do it? Well, I do at least get paid, but I like to be a sort of catalyst in their life. There is another reason, though. I raise funds for an Asian orphanage, so I encourage clients to support me and make regular donations. I've been doing this for a long time.

I set up the idea that I can 'stir their pot.' Encourage them to confront their past or even face their future. Whatever that may look like. Sometimes, they are just looking for a different direction in their life. I want to discover who they are, what they have done, and what secrets they may hold. You would be surprised.

My Clients

As their Chatter, I suspect that they feel my responsibility is to chat with them. To talk to them and help them to open up. Well maybe. There's certainly no way that I could just sit there waiting for them to talk to me. It's always up to me to initiate something.

To discuss a topic. Quite often, I become caught up in their personal issues. This is where things get interesting.

My technique? Well, it is easy, really, just be very gentle with them. But ask at the same time some probing questions that might make them sit back and think. For instance, when I entered Carol's life, I realised very quickly that there was something odd about her. About how she was living. The house was cold and lifeless. It certainly didn't feel that there'd been any love or comfort in the house. And the tea pots!! Who in the hell would have so many teapots?

I realised that this would be a hard nut that I would have to crack very gently.

I don't take any notes. I just listen and chat. When I arrive home, though, that's a different matter. I fill in my notebook quite quickly so as not to forget some interesting thoughts. Just so that I remember things about them. Sometimes, I may take a secret recording of our conversations. They would never know and honestly probably not care.

I also like to talk to them about becoming a sponsor of a child in the overseas orphanage that I support. Ask them to make a regular monthly donation so they can learn about the children, go to the website, and see the smiling faces. They like that, and I think it gives them a better idea about me.

The next time that I call around to see them, my usual start is to say, do you remember me? That may sound odd, but it helps me to get a handle on whether or not any memory loss is happening. Sometimes, a simple reminder like 'Last time we were chatting, you mentioned that ….' And then I remind them, and off they go. Chat, chat, chat and soon an hour has passed by.

I'd like you to meet one of my new clients. An interesting lady with what I feel may have been a troubled past. Her name is Carol Spicer.

Prologue

Carol Spicer

Carol came to me through a support service who refer a number of their clients to me. There are a number of such organisations in the area. Generally, they are set up to provide additional services to people on aged support or some other government support. Carol was receiving emotional and mental health support through a sort of health care package. That's part of how my income is derived.

I also have private clients. They are often referred to me by a social service, mental support services, or a psychologist. Sometimes, just by a friend. I like the private referrals. No government paperwork, just my contact.

When I think back, I thought that it would take me a while to get to know Carol. Whenever she was talking to me, she always seemed to be so distant, as if something was constantly on her mind. I wondered if there was something she was hiding from me or even making sure that she avoided answering any questions that may lead to the dark corner in which she seemed to be hiding. Or the issues that plagued her. Was there some hidden guilt or a disturbing family story? Who knows, but I was certainly about to find out.

I had found that with many of my clients, it was just necessary to ask some simple questions. To get them to talk, I wanted to understand them, to know where they were going in their life. And see if I could unearth some issues that plagued them.

It may well lead to a possibility of which I could take advantage.

There was no doubt that Carol's life had been a tough one. She displayed all of the patterns of a woman who had been mistreated. When I first met her, she certainly didn't want to shake hands with me. She just took me straight into her house and asked me if I wanted a cup of coffee or tea and asked me to sit down. None of the usual, 'Hello, how are you?' Hope you had a nice trip. Did you have trouble finding the house? Okay. None of the simple pleasantries that one might go through on meeting somebody for the first time. It was almost as if she didn't know how to respond to a stranger.

I knew I would have to be careful with how I treated Carol.

Carol Spicer grew up in the country near a small village outside of Fyfield in Essex. A small village where everybody just about knew everybody else. You would think that maybe if everybody knew your business and what was going on in the family, you may be quite annoyed or frustrated. But that really didn't seem to affect Carol and her family. They kept their stories…. Secret…. Very secret.

Her brother was not often seen in the village. It seems that after the incident, it was better that he stayed away. He had joined the army.

Carol had lived on the small farm all her life. She couldn't have been spoiled by her family. They didn't have enough money to spoil anybody. Carol remembered that Glen, her elder brother, moved away after the incident. Carol had little memory of him. The family thought it better that he be sent away to the army. So she was being brought up on her own, a bit like an only child.

Carol was seen as a gentle girl, attractive and kind. To some people, she may have seemed shy, but under her gentle exterior, I can tell you there must have been a strong, determined girl growing into a strong, determined woman.

She had a few friends at school and even stayed friends with them after she left. They would get together and spend some time developing friendships with the boys they knew from school. Carol really didn't seem to have time for most of the boys, and they seemed a bit immature. She was more interested in slightly older men, those who were more aware of life and what it could offer.

She knew about men and what they wanted. Unlike her girlfriends, who she hoped probably had no experience with men.

Unlike Carol and her family secrets. She remembered how her father would creep into her room at night, smelling of drink, and climb into her bed. He would tell her to keep quiet as he ran his hands all over her legs and onto her thighs, his horrible erection pressing into her. Then one night, she felt the pain as he pushed himself into her. She was only 14. She didn't remember any more until she woke up the next morning with her mother standing next to the bed.

Carol hated her father for what he had done and kept doing to her for a few years. She hated her mother for not stopping him and telling her to keep quiet about it. Life was hell for her. She was determined to move on and build a better future for herself. She was about 14 when it all started. Nearly every night.

Following the completion of her year 12 school experience, Carol began looking for a career position. Despite her sordid upbringing she had performed well in her studies and was considering moving on to a nursing course at her local Epping hospital. She felt there was the possibility of meeting an educated man, someone who knew about life. She felt that being a nurse may open up her life. Give her the opportunity to escape the confines of her home life. She would plan and wait and see. She had to go away.

Carol's Career

Life opened up for her. She was accepted by the hospital for a nurse's training course and managed to move into the nurse's quarters. After her course had completed, she found a small flat in Epping and lived there in what she felt was her own safe place. She grew into a capable, mature lady, qualified as a nurse, and was well-liked by the nurses on her wards. She had by now been a nurse for nearly 15 years. Life was full of learning with experiences that she found rewarding. The opportunity to share her tenderness with those who may be suffering. She had progressed to be a senior-level nurse.

When she finally met George, who was visiting a friend in her ward, she realised that she might have found a man with a deep sense of feeling, caring, and respect. He was certainly charming, confident, and attentive to her. Well, of course, nature was bound to take its course. Her heart gave way to him, and they soon established an intimate relationship. She hoped for something different than her father but maybe all men were just the same. Maybe he would mellow, she may have to show him what she wanted.

It didn't take long. Nearly 18 months later, they were married. Mr. and Mrs. George Mitchell set out to build their life together.

Chapter 1

Carol's Story

The Mirrors Reflection

It was 22 years after marrying George that Carol walked out of St. Mary's Church in High Ongar and down the path to the lychgate. She had left the car up near the Foresters Arms. She hesitated for a moment wondering if she should call in and have a toast to dead bastards. I'll do it later, she thought. I don't want to drink too much right now, especially as George didn't let me drink.

She shivered as she felt the winter winds blowing in her face. 'At last,' she murmured to herself, 'the bastard is dead and buried, and the bloody service is over. Now I can get home and start to build a better life.'

There had not been many people at the service. She didn't care. She didn't know any of those that were there anyway. Maybe they were people from his work or perhaps from the funeral company. Somehow, she didn't really care, and she just felt so happy.

She walked down the steps of the church as quickly as possible, wondering if there would be a feeling of emptiness. Would she have any feelings of guilt? Would she cope with being on her own? But somehow, she felt none of those things. Her life had been a bit that way anyway.

Why did her life go this way? Why didn't she realise what he was like? But that was the trouble. She thought to herself when she first met him, he was so charming, so confident, and attentive towards her. She was amazed at his job and how he was so important at work. That was why he was sent on the county jobs. Hah, that would soon show itself as a lie.

In the early days of their relationship, he was always telling their friends about how important he was and his wonderful achievements. She thought to herself, why didn't I see that this was all lies? Was I just caught up in his sense of his own importance?

Oh God, it makes me feel sick that I let him control me, but it was all too late. By the time I understood what was happening to me, I was utterly lost in his control and anger. He was clever. He didn't ever hit me, but harsh words can kill.

She walked slowly towards her car. She just wanted to go home and start her life all over again. All those wasted years of being married to him. Her life had been an utter waste. God, how she hated him for what he did to her. She wondered how she would ever be able to get her life back. To even trust someone. Somehow, get back into society.

She murmured to herself, 'Some years ago, that bastard of a man stole my life, and now I am so pleased that I have stolen his.'

Carol thought to herself. I never thought that love was supposed to be the way he made it feel ….. a constant push and pull, a game I could never quite win. He was the prize, and I, the willing participant, chased his approval like a dog chasing its tail. When did I become so small? So, willing to disappear?

I can't even remember the last time I looked in the mirror and recognised the woman staring back. Sometimes, I hated my reflection. I think he took her away, piece by piece, with every cutting word, every cold glance that told her she wasn't good enough. But today … Today, I feel something so …. different.'

I realise now what a narcissist he was. I was to find out the hard way that he had all the typical traits of a narcissist. Always believing he was more important than everyone else. He was always telling me about his so-called accomplishments at work. It was so embarrassing at social gatherings especially when we went for a drink at the local with friends. He would always turn the discussion to the things that he was planning to do.

Those friends slowly disappeared. All part of his bloody, controlling attitude. I remember hearing him on the phone one day, talking about what he was doing on his trips to Europe. That was just insane and such nonsense, and he didn't even go to Europe. I often looked for a passport or some airline ticket but never found one. Then he told people that he was a civil engineer. What a load of rubbish. He worked as a draftsman in an engineering office for the railways.

She was at last happy to be at home.

Carol remembered she knew exactly when that spark of anger had begun to grow in her. Maybe it was something even darker, something that whispered …… 'What if you just… stopped playing the game?'

The Moment of the Push

She smiled to herself as she thought about how easy it had been. A little push, and down the stairs, he went, breaking his neck in the fall.

The police were called in to carry out an interview. Sergeant Graham Williams from the Epping Police headed the interviews. At the inquest, George's death was put down to 'Accidental Death'. He had tripped, 'Hadn't he?' she said quietly to herself. After all, she was in the kitchen, 'wasn't she?' A happy little smile stretched across her face.

'I didn't plan it, did I? … Not really. Maybe it just grew inside me. But when I saw him standing at the top of the stairs, that smug, bloody look on his face, like he always knew I'd never leave…something inside me just snapped.'

My hands moved before my brain could catch up, shoving him with a force I didn't know I had. For a split second, time slowed down.

I could see the shock in his eyes the way his arms flailed as he tried to grab the banister. And then he was gone, tumbling down. The sound…God, the sound. It was like the world cracked open, and for a moment, I felt nothing but ….. I told myself it was an accident, he had tripped, and I just, I just couldn't stop him. I couldn't stop him. But deep down, I knew the truth. I didn't want to stop him.

The Aftermath.

I stood there, frozen, staring down at him. He didn't move. I couldn't tell if he was breathing, and I didn't want to check. Not yet. What had I done?

My heart was pounding in my chest, but it wasn't fear—not yet. It was something else, something that felt like relief or freedom. I couldn't let myself feel that. Not yet. Not when he was lying there, broken.

I will keep telling myself it was an accident. He had tripped, and I just… I just couldn't stop him, and I couldn't stop him. But deep down, I knew the truth. I had pushed him. I wanted him gone.

I really loved pushing him. And now he was gone….. I felt relief and heard nothing but ……. silence.

I let go of a small laugh .. 'I'll just have to live with that.'

I called the ambulance straight away. Luckily, the ambos arrived quite quickly. I didn't want to have his body lying on the floor for too long. I wanted him gone, out of the house. The senior ambulance officer reached and checked his pulse. Lifted his eyelids and flashed his torch beam into his eyes. He looked up at me. He walked over to me and took my hand. 'I'm so sorry, madam, but he has died. Do you have anyone?'

I answered quickly, didn't want him prying, 'No, not at the moment. I'll be OK.'

My heart raced. I could feel the blood pumping behind my eyes. My knees went weak. I let out a cry and sat on the stairs, crying into my hands. I wanted to scream …. with joy ….. Not yet…. My life was now my own. The bastard was dead…… The ambulance officers put him on the stretcher, quietly took him to the ambulance, and drove away. No sirens ..,. Just my laughter as the front door closed behind them.

The Inquest

Carol stood before the Coroner. She had rehearsed her explanation. Exactly what she had told the local police. She had learned how to cry. Consequently, the inquest was over quickly, with the 'Conclusion' being accidental death. Someone at the Court told her that it was a 'Jamieson Inquest,' which is why it was over quickly.

Due to her years in nursing, Carol knew what the Jamieson Inquest meant. It was a quick and uncomplicated Inquest. The Coroner will deal only with the four main questions that he or she has to deal with, namely, who died, where they died, when they died, and how they died. Because George's death was sudden and possibly violent, it was necessary to hold the Inquest. But it was over relatively quickly.

Carol had been questioned by the police but they seemed to know how it may have happened. I remember that one of the officers asked me if I reached out for him as he fell.

I simply said, 'No, I was in the kitchen.' Ha Ha, trick question. Saved, no panic, a simple response. I suspect he thought he might catch me out if I was lying. He didn't know me too well. I learned how to lie when I was a child.

I didn't care as long as I could get on with my life. George is dead and gone, and my life is ahead of me. Although Sergeant Graham Williams had a policeman's instinct that there was more to this than met the eye.

Post Inquest Paranoia

Even though the inquest was over, there was no doubt about it. Carol was having feelings that she may have a sort of paranoia.

I'm not sure if I am feeling happy or afraid. I don't feel that I can trust anybody at the moment. I certainly don't trust that police officer who threw that curly question at me, 'Did you reach out for him?' How could I? No, I was in the kitchen. Ha, answered him in a way that he must have been satisfied with my response; mind you, my instinct tells me not to trust him. But I was interviewed by the police a couple of times, and they seemed to be satisfied with my explanation. I was in the kitchen, cooking and George was coming downstairs. He was wearing the baggy 'around the house pants'; maybe he caught his foot, tripped, and fell down the stairs.

I don't have to worry, though, about family members. George had cut me off from my old friends and family, my children didn't talk to me, and I hadn't met his work contacts. Typical of a narcissist, and somehow it had really worked in my favour. But the hollowness that seemed to be within me now left me feeling confused, alone, and wondering if I needed some form of personal development that would help me prepare myself for the job market and polish up on my old skills. After all, it had been many years since I had actually worked.

George wouldn't let me work. He said there was no need for me to go to work. He would look after me. That felt good at the start. All I needed to do was look after him. Have his meals ready, wash his clothes, iron his work clothes. But slowly, that became monotonous and mundane. I realise now that it was all about his control over me.

It may have been enjoyable if I could have spent some time at home studying or doing a personal development course, which would have helped me get a job. But when I suggested that to George, he became angry and abusive, telling me that I didn't have the sense to do anything other than be a housewife. He just simply ignored the fact that I had studied nursing, or did he think that all I did was stick on plasters? God, I feel that I could k....., Carol stopped. She knew she had to stay calm. She didn't kill him .... He fell, he fell.

But now..... I am free to do whatever I want. Maybe I will go to a college after all and do a course on Mindfulness or Coping with Anxiety or something to help me move on a little stronger. Maybe the local UTC may have some courses.

The phone didn't ever ring, nobody called around to the house, the local people seemed to stay away, although I had never really met them. George wouldn't let me talk to them, not even the neighbours.

I'm worrying about nothing. I'm a widow now, and that's all that needs to be said. Besides, it's rude for people to pry.

The Grieving Widow

Carol realised that she had to play the part for a while. The grieving widow.

'I'll rebuild my life,' she thought. 'Try to look for work or do some volunteering, try to go back to nursing or try to re-establish connections with friends and family. I can start to go out more often, something that George would never let me do. HOLY HELL, WHAT WILL I DO?' She shouted.

Oh God, I really don't know what I want to do. I have to do something. I can't let this thought just linger in my mind. I have to…… Take my mind away from what happened.

As the days wore on Carol built up her courage and started to become a frequent visitor to the local sports club. She would sit alone and watch people. This was something totally new to her. To see how people acted together, to hear what they talked about. How they laughed. Now that was something new …. Laughing…. What was it that made you laugh? Over all the years that she had been married, laughing wasn't something that she did.

The staff were kind. Often asking me if I was OK. I'm fine, I would tell them.

I would watch the games. Or maybe just have a drink or two and listen to the pianist playing. Sometimes, I would cry gently to myself. But these were not tears of sadness. They were tears of joy. But those who sat near me couldn't tell. Tears are tears and sadness brings on tears.

Moving On

Back at home, Carol tried to find things to do. Things that a normal widow would do. She laughed to herself, 'How would I know what a normal widow would do?'

But even that was strange to her. Just what would a 'normal widow' do anyway?

She didn't feel like a sad, normal widow, and she felt elated, happy, and free.

She set about rearranging the house and furniture. Changing the place and getting rid of his bloody chair and the bloody stupid teapots that he collected. Fancy that, a grown man collecting teapots. She wanted to smash them onto the floor, but she thought, no, I'll give them to the 2nd hand Shop in town. She went out and bought the clothes that she wanted.

Not the clothes that he made her wear. She wanted colour, not dreary black. Sometimes, she just sat and watched television. Sometimes, she would try to read a book. But then she found her mind wandering, thinking that although she had her freedom, she was now becoming lonely or even bored.

It's no good, she thought to herself. I can't do this on my own. I need some guidance from a more professional person. I'll visit the UTC and see what they have. I need to do some studying, get my mind working again, and try to forget the years of mind-numbing hurt that I have gone through.

I really have no one to talk with or have a chat with. …Have a chat. Now that would be nice.

Carol would often find herself thinking about what her life had been like. She wasn't used to being lonely. Yes, maybe alone, but that was not the same. Admittedly, she didn't get much of a conversation from George. 'At least there was someone to talk to,' she thought to herself.

Carol looked at herself in the mirror. 'I am an attractive woman. I'm an attractive woman with a happy smile, and I have a good figure. I think I was like that too when I was married to

George. So why the abuse? Why did he treat me like that?'

I wondered why he behaved the way he did towards me. He seemed to change soon after we had our children and just stopped being loving and tender. Never seemed to really be affectionate after we were married. I had always hoped to be in a marriage where We could be intimate and enjoy ourselves together. But George never really cared about my needs. About how I was feeling.

I hated it when he would say to me, 'Go to bed and get ready. I'm coming up in a moment.' And I knew I would just have to put up with what he needed. The sex that he wanted. Nothing to do with the pleasure that I might want. God, it was horrible. I just lay there whilst he pushed himself into me and just grunted until it was all over. Luckily, that didn't take too long. I would get up and clean myself to get rid of his horrible smell.

I always wondered what it would be like to be with a man who could be affectionate. Tender. Loving. Care about what I wanted and how I felt. Now I wonder to myself. With my freedom, will I be able to ever trust another man?

Sadly, her children had not been at the funeral service or the inquest. They found it all too hard to come and visit. That was if they even knew. In fact, she wondered how they would know. Their upbringing must have left a scar on their emotions. Carol murmured to herself as she thought out loud, 'That was one of his narcissistic little treats. He had made sure that I was slowly separated from my children and the rest of my family, for that matter.'

She couldn't reach out to them when George was alive. She couldn't contact them. So naturally, the children thought that she just didn't want them anymore. She'll have to work on repairing that.

Oh, how sad it was. But it was not their fault. They were not to know. He had worked very cunningly to do this. He had denied her all those years. Now, they lived too far away. She would have to work out a way to slowly get them back into her life.

Maybe that was going to come quicker than she realised.

The Insurance Policy

The phone in the hallway rang. It made Carol jump. Nobody had called since the funeral.

She stood up and walked into the hall, almost afraid to pick up the phone. Two more rings, and she answered the call.

The caller was Kelvin Hunter, George's solicitor. 'Carol, I hope everything is going well. I'm calling to ask for your bank account details. The insurance company wants to pay the proceeds of George's life insurance policy into your account.'

Carol felt a wave of panic come over her. She only had one account and that was the account that George would use for her allowance.

'What insurance policy? I don't know anything about an insurance policy.' Carol answered with a tremble in her voice.

'George had a life insurance policy attached to his superannuation fund. You are the sole beneficiary,' Kelvin said in his assuring solicitor voice. 'A few days after the inquest when you were in my office. We submitted the paperwork. Maybe you were a bit … too sad … to remember. On George's death, you inherited the house and his superannuation fund. He wrote his will just after you were married and never reviewed or changed any part of it. You are the sole beneficiary.'

Carol thought quickly, remembering how when they were first married George had told her of his love for her and how he would look after her. He must have included her in his super fund and his Will. As he slowly turned into a rotten bastard, he must have forgotten to change things. But why did he forget? Was he going to change it later?

Did he think that he may not need to because … because she would die first…… Carol shivered all over. Was he going to kill me?

Carol wondered if it had been the business trips that he had been taking that perhaps took his mind off things. He did seem to be thinking about work a lot. Her mind started to swirl.

Carol read out the bank details to Kelvin and said goodbye. Just as she was about to hang up, she heard Kelvin call down the phone.

'Carol, Carol, don't you want to know how much George left you?' She thought for a moment.

'Oh, sorry, Kelvin, I was just a bit shocked. How much was it then?' Kelvin hesitated. 'Well, the superannuation balance is £243,876, and the life insurance is £435,493 so all up, it will be £679,369 plus the house. The insurances and superannuation may take a few days but you should have it in your account by next Friday. Please call me if you have any problems or need any investment advice.'

Kelvin paused for a moment as he put the phone down. He thought to himself. 'Well, maybe it really was an accident after all.'

Carol put the phone down very slowly as if it would make any difference. She was stunned. The money, My God, the money was finally there, close to what she had seen when she opened the recent letter from the superannuation company. She didn't know about the Will and the house, though.

'But I didn't do it for the money.' She smiled to herself, 'But I suppose that is the value of my freedom.'

Carol sat at the kitchen table. She needed to plan how to use or invest the money.

The phone rang again. Carol didn't want to answer it this time. She waited until the answering machine started. 'Hello, Mrs Mitchell. This is Sergeant Williams from the Epping police station. I hope you are well. I wanted to call in and see you just as part of our support follow up. Would you please call back when convenient? Thank you.'

Carol's heart began to beat fast. No rush. I'll make sure to cover up any loose ends.

Time to Chat

The Chatter arrives

Time had passed in Carol's life. Things had settled down except for the recent phone call. Money in the bank and house in her name. She had seen some courses that she could do at Evening College, but they started in a few months' time.

In the meantime, Social Services had recommended the connection with a local Chatter. She had enrolled in the services of a local Chatter, having finally got to a point when she realised that she needed to at least have the services of someone to talk to …. a Chatter. Somebody she could talk with. Just generally. Have an uncomplicated discussion. A friendly chat. She liked to think of it like that.

The big issue in her mind? Could she avoid ever bringing up the issue of George? Of how her husband George had died. She knew that the only way to convince herself that it was an accident was to keep telling herself that it was an accident: he fell, he fell, he fell. Yes… he fell. It was an accident. The more I tell myself the lie, the closer it comes to the truth, and the closer I come to believing it,

There was a knock at the front door. Carol stood up. With a bit of luck, this would be the Chatter. She had been expecting her arrival sometime this morning.

She opened the door. 'Hello, I'm Jean. I'm your Chatter. Hopefully, the office called you to confirm that I was coming. May I come in?'

Carol quickly looked Jean up and down. She had never had a Chatter before. If this is her Chatter, then she knew that she had to have an instinctive liking and be confident right from the very start. If she wasn't very comfortable with the new Chatter standing there, then it would probably never work.

Her mouth felt a little dry, and she had a few trembles in her back, but Carol felt safe so far.

'Of course, you can come in. Please leave your shoes at the front door. Come into the lounge and take a seat. Would you like a cup of coffee or tea, perhaps, before we sit down and start our chat?' Carol gave a small chuckle. Jean answered, 'A white tea, please, no sugar,'

Jean cast her eyes over the room and then up and down Carol as she walked in and took a chair. Wow, the house seemed to have a strange air about it. Almost a bit cold. She couldn't see any photos or pictures on the wall, which was a bit strange for a lady who's living here on her own. Carol seemed to be a little bit tense. Almost as if she was unsure of what to do.

Jean tried to assess Carol. She had learned to make a quick assessment of a new client, trying to work out how to plan the session and see where it may go. She looked. Bare feet, how odd for an English lady to do that. How odd. I wonder why she does that.

What Jean didn't know, although she may find out soon, was that it was George's requirement. Carol knew why George made her take off her shoes. Simple. If she tried to run out of the house she wouldn't get far in bare feet. But now that had turned into Carol's habit.

Jean still wondered to herself if she was going to be able to have a pleasant chat. It wasn't always easy chatting with some of the older clients. Oh well, she thought, just remember the orphanage.

Jean turned to Carol and started to explain how 'The Chat' could go. She would simply ask a few questions about Carol's life, places she may have visited, or even her views on matters affecting her life, such as the internet and so on.

Jean thought she would talk about using social media. Eventually, she may get around to asking if Carol is on any dating websites. Jean would share some of her thoughts, too. At some point, she wanted to introduce the orphanage to see if Carol would like to become a supporter of one of the children.

When Jean mentioned the internet, Carol laughed inside. There was no internet in her life; George would never have allowed that. Since his recent death she hadn't bothered, although she may ask Jean about it.

Jean started 'The Chat.' 'Why not tell me about your childhood and early life memories to start with. Jean sat and listened as Carol began to tell her life story. Carol started by talking about the farm. What her life was like. The village people.

The gossiping. She didn't talk about the family secrets, though.

When Carol stopped talking, Jean realised that she needed to get a closer understanding. What had been Carol's past. So using the direct approach that Lizbeth had shown her, Jean spoke. 'What was your relationship like with your parents?'

For a moment, Carol felt very odd. I didn't want to discuss that, she thought. Carol looked at Jean for a moment. 'Why did you ask that?'

Jean wasn't surprised, 'Well, I notice that you don't have any pictures or photos of your parents or your children or even your husband. Most of my clients seem to have family memories on the sideboard or have something on the wall. For instance, your husband or parents or maybe your children, even a pet or two. Your application mentioned that you were married and had two children. I wondered if you have any photos. Upstairs perhaps or in another room?'

Carol felt cold for a moment. Photos? It felt as if George was coming back to haunt her. Photos. I never thought about that. George never let me put photos on the wall. He didn't want me to see my family members, that would annoy him. He only wanted images of me, but even so, there weren't any photos!!

'I never was a great one for wall hangings, and my photos are in an album.' Carol spluttered out. 'Just more dust carriers, as far as I'm concerned.'

Jean watched as Carol seemed to be a bit uncomfortable. Jean thought to herself that she needed to find out who else may be a part of Carol's family group. Certainly, more about her life. Jean just waited. Watching the look on Carol's face.

Jean realised that she may have touched the nerve that was going to get Carol to open up. This is an older lady living in a large house. Is she on her own, and how did she end up here? Why no photos? All too odd for me….. But maybe an opportunity.

Jean could feel that there was something more to discover about Carol, but she needed to touch that nerve again to get her to talk more… much more. What had happened to her husband?

Jean decided that she needed to ask some more direct questions. The more questions she asked the more likely Carol would be to blurt things out. Firstly, about Carol's husband. She took a small breath. 'Carol, would you mind telling me a bit tell me about your husband, how you get on, how you feel about your relationship with him? Where do all the teapots come from, and who is the collector?'

Carol sat back in her chair. She knew this would happen one day, someone would ask.

So she had to tell. This was her Chatter, after all. She could feel the drips of perspiration running down her back.

'I don't know where to start really. I suppose that I should tell you that George died a few months ago. He fell down the stairs and broke his neck. He was dead when the ambulance arrived. It was a case of accidental death. He was walking around in his old baggy pants when he must have caught his foot and fell. After the inquest, I tried to get my life back together. My life has been hell. He was an utter narcissist. That's the real reason that there are no pictures on the wall. He wouldn't allow me to have any signs of my children. I haven't seen them for years. I don't have any friends, and my children don't see me.

I am so in need of friendship, trying to get my life back together, it's so hard. That's why I need you. My Chatter. '

Jean couldn't believe such a simple question had opened up the floodgates. Lizzie Hurley had always said it would. She felt very excited to hear those words, 'I need You.' Well this was going to be a little bit easier than I thought. I'll introduce the orphanage sooner than I thought.

'Carol, there is something that I would like to ask you. For some years now I have been supporting an orphanage in Cambodia. I was wondering if you would like to become a supporter?'

Chapter 2

Evelyn's Story

The Tea and the Tulips

Prologue

Evelyn Archer grew up in a loving family. Mum and Dad helped both her and her brother, Jason, to grow and develop into caring people. You may have imagined that life was a bed of roses for Evelyn Archer, but far from it. Evelyn's Dad had been confined to a wheelchair since his car accident some 5 years before Evelyn finished school. But he was still there at the Speech Night when she received her Top Student of the School award. In her Awards Speech she would mention how her parents had taught her to be truthful and lend a hand to those less fortunate than themselves.

Evelyn's friends were always visitors to her home.

The Writing Career

Ever since she was in High School, Evelyn had wanted to be a writer, a journalist preferably, who would tell the stories of everyday people, the unsung heroes who share their lives to help others, the volunteers who are always there to lend a hand.

Her career really started at High School where she found herself as the Editor of the School magazine, writing stories about students and interviewing teachers to discover what motivated them to teach. What a way to learn about your fellow students and teachers!

After submitting her resume and going through the interviews with the Editor and others on the selection panel, Evelyn finally received the good news that she had been waiting for. She had been selected for the Cadet Journalist role. So now here she was, on the way to …… she didn't quite know where, but she would know when she got there.

What luck. She soon found herself on the Court reporting schedule, making regular visits to the Magistrates Court. A whole raft of misdemeanours on which to report. Minor traffic infringements, shoplifting, disorderly behaviour. Sometimes assaults, burglary, drug offences, and even cattle theft. .

Evelyn always took her work seriously to prove to the newspaper editor that she was ready to move up to being a regular reporter. In her role as a reporter, she knew that objectivity was the focus. She wasn't there to pass opinions, just the facts. Report the facts. She also had an idea for a series of articles that would increase readership. But her life was about to change.

One day as she walked into the Magistrates Court, she happened to see Michael Parker. A local solicitor who was always available to help or represent some of the 'naughty boys before the beak.'

'Michael, sorry to bail you up, pardon the pun, but I wondered if we could catch up after your last appearance today? I need to have a word with you.'

'That sounds nice, but who are you?' he replied with a quizzical look on his face. It wasn't often that he was 'bailed up' by a rather attractive lady, and this one looked very attractive to him.

'Sorry, …..there I go …. apologising again… I'm Evelyn Archer, a reporter for the Daily News. Actually mainly Court reporting at this stage, but things are getting better as I get better. I would like to talk to you about an issue that troubles me.'

'OK. How about The Tea Shop, 4.30?' 'Wonderful, thank you.' Replied Evelyn. 'See you then.' Evelyn turned and went to sit at the tables where the 'Press' sat.

The Meeting

Sitting at the table Evelyn looked at Michael, thanking him for meeting with her. The conversation that she wanted to hold centred on his apparent willingness and approach to helping people. 'You seem to be so willing to help and support people. Why?'

'Is this a general chat or 'for the record, Ms Court Reporter…...'

'Well, I did want to ask you if I could write an exposé on your role. Would that be OK?'

'I think that would be fine, although I may have to check with the boss.'

'I want to write a series of articles on 'People in our Place.'

'That sounds interesting… get to know the people. Well, it's part of my role, really, but at the same time, I do feel sorry for some of those so-called offenders. I was fortunate to have a good life as I grew up. My dad was a lawyer, so it seemed a natural move for me to follow in his footsteps. But as I grew into the job and met some of the offenders, I began to realise that there was a bit more to their situation. I suppose to put it in a summary, they seemed to have little in the way of personal direction or goals.

They lacked any drive. It's not their fault, really. I suppose if you don't get that as you grow up, then it is not just a matter of knowing right from wrong or setting goals and objectives. If you give them a fine, then you take away their support; if you jail them, then they get a record, and that ruins their future. But if you could work with them to 'build a better future,' then you may set them straight.'

'Wow, Michael, that is carrying a torch for the less fortunate. Maybe you should go into politics?'

'Not really, it's about building a better society.'

Evelyn had taken copious notes. So it was now back to her editor with a plan to start 'People in our Place,' a series of interviews…. Just like the old-school magazine.

'Thank you, Michael, that was a wonderful insight into you.' Before they parted Michael suggested that they should meet again sometime. Evelyn agreed, not realising they had just made their first date. Evelyn Asher would soon become Mrs Evelyn Parker.

Chapter 2
The Tea and Tulips
Evelyn's story

The Lonely Garden

Evelyn Parker, now in her early sixties, is a woman of quiet grace. Her days are spent in a small, picturesque cottage in her village of High Laver in Essex, surrounded by a garden she had lovingly nurtured for years. The tulips, her favourite flowers, stand proudly in their beds, vibrant and alive. Evelyn's life, however, was far less colourful now.

Widowed at fifty, Evelyn had been alone for over a decade. Her marriage to Michael had been a good one, filled with the familiar comforts of a long-term partnership. But since his passing, loneliness had crept in like a persistent fog, blurring the edges of her once-clear sense of self. Evelyn missed their intimacy, those morning moments when they would make love. She could still remember his arms holding her tightly as she reached the peak of her orgasm. They were both still sexually active. Oh, how she missed him and their intimacy.

She regretted not having children, but she and Michael had taken the decision to dedicate their lives to helping those less fortunate. It was a mutual decision that resulted in a wonderful journey to creating happiness for others. Would she change that decision today? Oh yes. She had thought of adopting or supporting an orphanage.

She was not old, but she wasn't young either, yet she found herself longing for something— or someone— to fill the void. She would look at herself in the mirror, wondering if she was still a woman that a man would like to make love to in her bed.

Evelyn had always been independent, but as the years passed, she yearned for companionship. She missed the warmth of a hand in hers, the comfort of a voice that wasn't just her own. She wasn't looking for love, necessarily, but the idea of a male lover or friend, someone who could bring a bit of light and laughter back into her life, began to take root in her mind.

A Chance Encounter

Evelyn's routine visits to the town market were the highlight of her week. She enjoyed the bustle, the small talk with the vendors, and the simple pleasure of choosing fresh produce. It was on one such visit that she noticed a man she had never seen before.

George Mitchell appeared to be in his mid-sixties, with a full head of silver hair and a rugged handsomeness that spoke of a life well-lived. He was perusing the tulips at the flower stall, his large hands carefully selecting a bouquet. Something about his demeanour

……. the way he studied the flowers as if each one held a secret …..caught Evelyn's attention.

'They're beautiful, aren't they?' Evelyn said, her voice breaking the silence between them.

George looked up, meeting her gaze with a smile on his face that reached his eyes. 'They certainly are. Tulips have always been my favorite.'

'They're mine too,' Evelyn replied, feeling a warmth she hadn't expected.

They began to walk and talk, first about the flowers, then about the town, and finally, about their lives. George told her that he had recently moved near Epping. He was still working in his career as a civil engineer. He travelled a lot, and although he had lost his wife a few years earlier, he was now seeking a quieter life, a place where he could find some peace.

Before they parted, George suggested they should have tea together sometime. There was a gentleness in his offer, an unspoken understanding that resonated with Evelyn's intimate longing. She hesitated for only a moment before agreeing.

The Blooming

Their first tea was a simple affair in Evelyn's garden. They sat beneath the shade of an old oak tree, surrounded by the tulips that had just begun to bloom. George was easy to talk to, his voice smooth and reassuring. They spoke of books, travel, and the peculiarities of growing older. There was a chemistry between them, subtle but undeniable.

As the weeks passed, their meetings became more frequent. Evelyn found herself looking forward to George's visits, her heart fluttering in a way she hadn't felt in years. It wasn't just companionship she was seeking anymore; it was something more intimate, deeper, something she hadn't dared to hope for since Michael's death.

One evening, as they sat together on her front patio porch watching the sunset, George reached out and took her hand. The touch was gentle but deliberate, sending a thrill through Evelyn's body. She turned to him, her eyes searching his face for answers.

'Evelyn,' George began, his voice low and serious, 'I think you know that I've grown very fond of you. More than I ever expected.'

Evelyn's breath caught in her throat. She had sensed this moment was coming, but now that it was here, she wasn't sure what to say. She felt the same way. She wanted to call out 'Yes!' but there was something in George's tone that caused her to pause.

'I feel the same,' she admitted, her voice barely above a whisper. 'But…is this what you really want?' Why did I say that, she wondered. I want him so much.

George looked towards her, his expression clouded with something Evelyn couldn't quite read. When he turned back to her, there was a sadness in his eyes that hadn't been there before.

'I care about you very much, Evelyn,' he said slowly. 'But there's something you should know. I didn't come here just for the peace and quiet. I've been searching for something—something I lost when my wife passed. I hoped that I could find it here, but… I'm not sure if it is what you may want. You see, my work takes me away quite often, and our office has contracts all over.

Sometimes, I may be away for two or even four weeks at a time.

Would you miss me if I was away that long?'

Evelyn felt a chill run through her. 'Oh George, you are so silly. Of course, I would miss you, but I would wait for you forever. I will always wait to feel you near me. What are you asking George?'

'I'm saying that while I care for you deeply, I don't want to take you away from someone who may be able to stay with you longer. I'm searching for something that I think I've found, but I just don't want to lose you,' he replied, his voice tinged with passion.

'I didn't mean for this to happen, for us to grow so close, so soon. I just…I know that I'm ready for this kind of relationship with you.'

The words hung between them, gentle and wrapped in a beautiful sensuality. Evelyn squeezed George's hand. She felt the tears roll down her cheeks. She knew she wanted him. She had opened her heart, and she didn't want to lose him. She was faced with the reality that both she and George could be as one. Her heart was beating. No, she didn't want to lose him either. She felt the love and desire within her, and she hoped that George would deliver that to her as well.

'Don't go, George, sleep with me tonight.'

A Garden in Bloom

The days that followed were wonderful for Evelyn. She continued to see George whenever he could be there with her. It was his work that took him away but there was sometimes a distance between them that hadn't been there before. Their conversations were still pleasant, funny, and they laughed, their time together still enjoyable, but the unspoken feelings were ever-present.

One day, as they walked through the village together, George paused by a small shop window. Inside, a beautiful ceramic teapot was displayed, its design reminiscent of the ones Evelyn had admired in her youth.

'What do you think?' George asked, his tone light but his eyes still glinting with love. Evelyn smiled sweetly. 'It's lovely.' George turned to her, his expression softening. 'Let me get it for you. A gift for all the wonderful teas we've shared.' Evelyn hesitated. She appreciated the gesture, but she knew that no teapot could hold the growing love between them. Still, she nodded, allowing him this small kindness.

As time went by, Evelyn and George's relationship settled into a comfortable rhythm. They were lovers, companions, and friends. Perhaps something more—but not exactly what Evelyn had hoped for….. yet. She learned to accept that George was still thinking about his work, seemingly planning for whatever it was he needed, but perhaps his journey might soon conjoin with hers in the way she had imagined.

Yet, despite the uncertainty, Evelyn found peace in their relationship. She realised that life, much like her garden, was ever-changing. Not all blooms were meant to last, but that didn't mean they weren't beautiful while they did.

And so, in the quiet town where the tulips bloomed every spring, Evelyn continued to nurture her garden and her beautiful, intimate friendship with George. The path ahead might be unclear, but she knew that as long as she had her garden, her memories, and the companionship of a good man, she would be all right.

She rolled over and put her arms around George, kissing him on his neck. He was such a gentle and loving man. She wanted him so much.

The Coldness of Winter

Evelyn began to wonder when she might hear from George. It had been two weeks since his last call. He did say that he would be away for at least 4 weeks on this trip, but he would often call her if he was away on a long trip. She hoped that he was OK. She missed him so much.

She was finding the coldness of winter almost too hard to take with no George beside her. The garden was looking bleak, but it was winter after all. She couldn't wait for Spring and the Tulips and George to be with her.

She reminded herself that he had told her a couple of times that there was no point in calling him. He had told her that, quite often, there was no mobile reception in the places in which he was working and gently assured her that if anything happened, then the London office would contact her straightaway. He had even put her name down as his personal contact. That made her feel so good. She felt that at least he had shown signs that he loved her.

Evelyn sat near the log fire in her cottage. She watched the flames dancing along the timber as she thought about George. It was nearly four weeks, and she had not heard a word from George. No emails, nothing. She thought about calling the London office only to realise that she didn't actually have the number or the name of the company.

Although she had developed a wonderful loving relationship with him, she had, luckily, still kept in contact with Jean, her Chatter. They would now only meet once a month. They used to meet every fortnight, but since she had met George, a once-a-month chat was enough. She enjoyed the time with Jean. There was a sort of synergy with her. A certain openness in how they talked to each other.

The next time they met she decided that she would still talk about her past and now, more so, her future, especially how she was feeling about George, the man in her life. She would still continue to give her the money for the orphanage, though.

Evelyn's anxiety continued to grow. She had not heard from George for several, oh she didn't know how long anymore, she just knew that it had seemed endless. She called Jean to make an appointment. 'I need to Chat with you as soon as possible. How soon would you be able to get here?'

'Well, I can come today. Probably, subject to traffic, in about 2 hours. What is the matter, Evelyn?'

'It's George. He told me that he was going away for a few weeks, but I have heard nothing from him at all. No calls. Nothing.

I'm feeling sick with worry. Please come soon.'

Jean tried to add a few reassuring words and told her she was on her way. This trip will take a good 2 hours, she thought to herself. I need her in a bit of a state when I get there.

The Chatter Arrives

Jean pulled up outside Evelyn's house. She wasn't quite sure of what was going to happen, but she realised that somehow she needed to make sure that Evelyn did all the talking. Talk about how she was feeling, how she was missing George, what she would like to happen with their relationship, anything really so that she could work out just what had happened as well as concoct a sort of solution. At best, the story needed to be strung out.

On the drive over to Evelyn's cottage, she had begun to wonder just how likely it was that Evelyn's George was possibly more than likely Carol's George, too. There were too many coincidences. Both Georges were civil engineers, and both seemed to travel away for work, and both said that their relationship was so good. Although Carol spoke about the start and how it went downhill, Evelyn hadn't really had time to experience the downhill slide into narcissism. Luckily for her. She still maintained that feeling of having a new lover.

Jean wasn't sure how she felt about all of this. She realised that it would be necessary to get on top of the situation. What should she say to Carol? Should she say anything at all? The same applied to Evelyn. Should she say anything? At least she could gain some more funding for her 'private detective' work.

Jean realised that tonight she would at least pick up a 'fee for service' to meet the payment for the 'out of scheduled Chat,' plus the ongoing contribution to the overseas orphanage. That was a real money spinner especially as she had now met Carol and Angela.

There was also the chance that maybe she would be able to charge a fee to do some 'private investigation work.' But that would be 'money for jam' as she realised that she probably already knew the answer! The issue will be how long she can keep it going. Would she ever explain the issue to Evelyn, and how can she talk to Carol? Should she let them meet? This felt a bit exciting to Jean.

Jean stepped out of the car and walked up to Evelyn's front door. She picked up the knocker and made two knocks. Evelyn opened the door before the echo had rung down the hallway!

Jean looked at Evelyn. The poor lady looked like death. Oh, thought Jean, that's not quite the description I should use, bearing in mind George's probable demise.

'Oh, thank heavens you made it in good time. Come on in, and I'll make you tea. Take a seat, and I'll be with you in a minute.'

Jean sat down, very aware of the stress that Evelyn must be going through. 'Evelyn, just what is it? Please tell me.'

'Well, it's George, or should I say the lack of George.' Evelyn sat down next to Jean. 'He hasn't been in touch with me, for I expect 4 weeks or more, I don't know. I didn't realise how much I want him, Jean, and I'm feeling sick without him near me! He has changed my whole life, and now it has all stopped. I want to hold him. I need him to make love to me.'

Jean tried to take in just how Evelyn must be feeling right now. Here was this sweet lady, a widow for a decade who had fallen in love with a man who had lifted her into a happiness that she had forgotten. Right, let's start with basic questions, thought Jean.

'OK Evelyn, let's start with a few basic questions or two. First, do you have his mobile number and the name of his employer or his company and, importantly, his email address?'

Evelyn held her head in her hands. Jean sighed, and Evelyn burst into tears. 'Evelyn, who did he work for, or was he self-employed? How did you contact him?'

Evelyn let out a deep sigh, 'He always rang me. He said he couldn't talk for long as the contact line was used by other company staff. He could be out of reach or the internet contact was poor. His line kept breaking up, and sometimes we were cut off. I just wanted to hear his voice and hear how he said he loved me. Oh, Jean, I just want to scream. I am so afraid that something may have happened to him.'

Jean tried not to let it show, but she just wanted to say,

'HE'S DEAD.'

Instead, she said nothing, realising that opportunity knocked.

After those few words from Evelyn, Jean decided that she would not say anything to either Carol or Evelyn. They need never know and she would continue to profit from them.

'Evelyn, there's a few things that I can do for you. First, let me look at your phone to source his call locations. I can carry out some investigations, but I'll have to charge a fee as it will take me some time, and more than likely, I will need to pay some people to give me information. Are you OK with that?'

Evelyn nodded; she was so desperate that she would have said yes to anything. 'This meeting will be at the normal rate, but we can catch up again as soon as I have some information for you.

Is 50 to start OK?' Evelyn nodded and went to her room to get the cash.

'Now I want you to relax, take deep breaths, and think about a good outcome. I'll be in touch in a couple of days, but whatever you do please call me if you are feeling at all upset.'

Jean left Evelyn sitting on the couch as she went back to her car, 500 pounds in hand and feeling quite elated. Well, it's certainly George, she thought, married to one and having an affair with the other. This was not going to end well. How it would end, she didn't know, but she knew it wouldn't end well.

Chapter 3
The Hallowed Halls of Education
Angela's Story
Prologue

Dr. Angela Groves, PHD had just turned 55. She is still single, with no attachments either. She struggles as she attempts to navigate her career and personal life. She has spent much of her life dedicated to her career. She is a respected person in her field of psychology and sociology, being subjects that seem to align with her introspection and self-reflection. Whilst successful professionally, her personal life is marked by isolation, unresolved emotional wounds, and a deep personal internal conflict. This may be a slightly troubled lady.

During her younger years, she had often had feelings for women, but she brushed them aside, convincing herself that they were just 'a close friendship.'

She did have some men friends when she was an undergraduate, but these were more out of societal expectations rather than genuine desires, but they never seemed to fulfill her inner desires. Whatever those feelings were, she didn't know, and she sometimes wondered if she was even the relationship type.

Her constant introspection made her realise that she may well have buried her feelings so deeply that she missed the chance for true connections because she was too afraid to accept who she really was. But she hoped that one day she may meet someone who will cause her to confront her feelings and totally change how she sees herself. After all, many of her lesbian students lived an openly lesbian life.

She had never aligned herself with the lesbian movement or LGBTQ groups; rather, she just accepted her sexuality, preferring to put her energies into her work.

Angela realised what she may have lost in sacrificing her personal life for her academic achievements; however, she knew the importance of constant publishing, creating innovative research, and bringing fees to the university, which is always useful for her future. She had turned her work towards providing social research studies and trying to identify patterns in social life.

She wanted to focus more on interpersonal and family breakdowns. Her focus group studies would be drawn from studies through 'support groups in specific community groups.'

Angela knew that whilst she may present as a confident and knowledgeable person she was indeed lonely. Her home life was empty, and she lived in a small flat full of books and papers. She seemed to watch the world from a distance.

Deep inside, she felt that the moment she met someone special, she would know. The turning point would be beyond wonderful.

Dr. Angela's story

The Focus Group

Dr. Angela had a connection with a local UTC [University Technical College], which enabled her to run a focus group in their rooms. She utilised social media to find appropriate people to join in, which didn't seem to take long to attract attendees with the background she needed. Angela's Master's students at the uni were all too keen to help screen the applicants and set up the groups.

Following her search for a support group, Carol had come across a local UTC Focus Group being run by the local university. Dr Angela Groves, a lecturer in Sociology at Essex University in Colchester, wanted to do a study on family breakdowns.

'Well, I wonder if my husband's death will be considered a family breakdown?' Carol asked herself, laughing.

When Carol called the contact number, she found herself being asked a series of initial screening questions. All good. She passed the initial test questions. The person on the phone then invited her to attend the Focus Group. Carol agreed to attend the next focus group where she would receive a payment at the end of the session. It would take about two hours. She didn't need the money, really, but would accept it anyway. Her first real 'income' since she married George.

As she was heading back home, she smiled to herself, 'God, how my life has changed already. 'Not so long ago, I didn't have any money. Now…. Well, I have plenty, but I do wonder why that police officer, Sgt Williams had called. Part of the police support follow up he said. That sounded like a bit of a made-up excuse. She would leave the return call for a while.' She had more pressing meetings to respond to.

The next day, Carol found her way to the lecture room where Dr. Angela Groves was holding the focus group. She knocked on the door and walked in. 'Hello' come on in.' Angela proffered her hand. Angela realised that she was looking at Carol in a very different way than she had looked at any of the other ladies who had entered the study room that day. A handshake would at least establish that first contact, she thought.

Carol reached out and shook hands, noticing that Angela held on for a few seconds longer than normal. It felt nice. The first real touch of another person since George had died.

Carol sat and listened as Angela explained the reason for the focus group, the use of the data that she would collect, and how the results would be used and remain totally confidential.

The questions seemed quite harmless to start with, yet

Carol began to feel as if Angela was speaking just to her, one-to-one as if she was the only person in the room. Mind you there had to be 12 others there at least. Carol started to read the questions. They seemed so personal….

1. On a scale of 1-5 on the scale below, show how true it is that family life may benefit men more than women.

2. On a scale of 1-5 on the scale below, show how family life may disadvantage women's careers.

3. Using one of the answers below show how there may be a loss of Childhood in Contemporary Society. Carol suddenly felt cold. This reminded her of her childhood, the family secret.

4. Select from one answer to briefly explain why women may choose to postpone having children until they are older.

Carol felt cold. She suddenly began to feel as if she was being interrogated by the 'thought police.' Her whole life was in those questions. Everything pointed to what had happened to her from childhood 'till today.

She could write a paper on her life and answer every question.

This made her feel terrible. She began to feel weak and a bit shaky. Almost as if she was going to faint. Dr Angela Groves had been looking towards Carol most of the session and suspected that something was wrong. Carol was flushed and seemed to be breathing too fast.

Angela went over to her, 'Are you OK, Carol? You look a bit overwhelmed. Is everything OK?'

Carol sat back in her chair. 'Dr Groves, I need to talk to you. I need to call Jean. She is my Chatter. It's important. I need to talk to you, too. These questions are about my life. I don't know what to do right now.'

Angela looked at Carol, 'Let me get you some water. Can you explain what you mean, what is a Chatter? Where do you live? Do you have anyone at home, or can I take you home?'

Carol listened to the barrage of questions as she slowly seemed to come back to her normal senses. Her pulse slowed down. She didn't know where to start as she wondered what had happened to her.

She knew that she wanted to speak to Jean. Some of the discussions that she had started with Jean were beginning to make sense. No pictures on the walls, no friends, no job, but all of a sudden, plenty of money. The phone call from Sgt. Williams. She needed to open up to Jean.

Carol looked up at Dr. Groves, 'Would you mind taking me home? I can fetch my car tomorrow.'

'That's OK. I think I should stay with you tonight, make sure that you are ok. I'll explain to your husband.'

'I don't have a husband. He died, I'm a widow.' A strange feeling instantly seemed to flood through Angela.

'Oh, I'm sorry to hear that.'

'Don't be, I'm glad the bastard died.'

'Come on, I'll take you home.'

Chapter 4
Glen Spicer's Story

The Early Years

Glen and his sister Carol had grown up on the farm in Fyfield together. Although Glen was 5 years older than Carol, he still didn't leave home until he was 19.

His family life was violent, with a father who would be described as a loathsome man with no love for his children. Life for Glen was turbulent, to say the least. As he grew up, he felt the strap for any misdemeanour or the back of his father's hand, wherever it landed. There were days when Glen couldn't go to school due to the bruises on his face. It was a torrid life for a boy who was, without doubt, gentle and caring.

At the age of four, Glen witnessed the first of the beatings his mother would receive from his father. She could never fight back as he was a big man. Glen would run and hide in the cattle food sheds to get away from the screams. He would cover his ears while his poor little body was wracked with distress, and tears rolled down his face.

As he grew up, he hated those nights when his father would come home, smell of drink, and go into his sister's room. It was only a few years later, after he had joined the army that he really understood what was happening to Carol. Glen wanted to kill him.

The Army

Glen had left school when he reached 17. He knew that he had to get away from the farm. His life had been awful, and he just wanted to start all over again, be somewhere to make friends, and probably travel overseas. For him he saw the Army as his only way out. One of the soldiers who had visited his school talked about the introductory year in the army to help students learn about army life and gain an idea of what they could do once they joined up.

Glen felt excited about the thought of being able to get involved in transport. He could already drive, having learned to drive the tractors on the farm. Not only that, but he would be paid too! The other thought was that when he left the army he may be able to work driving trucks. He also wondered if he would ever leave the army.

The Traumatic Memory

Glen had suffered beatings from his father as he was growing up, but try as he might, he could not repress the memory of that dreadful day. He would remember that he had decided to take a shortcut over the fields to his home. He had to walk down the bank of the River Roding to the footbridge, cross over, and then walk back up the other side towards the Spicer's farm.

As he crossed over the footbridge, he heard a stifled shout coming from within the trees. He stopped to listen in case there was another cry out. As he stared into the undergrowth he felt sick at what he saw.

It was his father and what looked like a young girl rolling in the grass. It seemed as if she was trying to get up, but his father was laying on top of her, holding her down as he was pulling her dress off.

Glen panicked and ran. If his father saw him, he knew that he would be in for a severe beating. He realised that he was raping the girl, whoever she was, he couldn't tell, but his life was too valuable to risk trying to stop his father.

He just hoped it wasn't Carol.

Glen ran home straight into the cattle feed sheds. He sat panting and feeling very afraid. He didn't know what to do or how to hide from his father. Quite soon, a beam of light pierced the dust-filled air as his father opened the shed door. He knew where Glen would go when he was having a panic attack.

Pulling his broad leather belt from his pants, he walked towards Glen. 'If you don't want this across your back, you had better go and join that Army you have talked about and stay away from here. You know nothing, and you saw nothing. Go tomorrow.'

Glen knew that he had to move away quickly. The following morning, he appeared at the recruitment office in Epping. Standing in line to lodge his application forms, school leaving forms, and letters from his doctor confirming that he was physically fit and healthy. He was told that the confirmation of his application would be mailed to him very soon. Glen knew that it couldn't come quickly enough!

He was looking forward to the trip to Catterick Garrison in Yorkshire, as far away as possible from the beatings.

Leaving Home

With the arrival of the letter from the Army, Glen collected his clothes as had been outlined by the Army and hugged his mother goodbye, holding on to her long enough for her to know that he knew. He turned to his little sister, looking her in the eyes. He grabbed her tightly and whispered to her. She smiled and held Glen tightly, too. Tears flowed from each of them.

There was no sign of Glen's father. Thank God, he said to himself.

Glen headed out to wait at the bus stop where the Army bus would pull up. He said a slow and sad goodbye to Fyfield. 'I'll be back one day.'

Glen knew that he had no idea of what lay ahead but he did not worry. As far as he was concerned, his life was about to turn around.

Chapter 5

The Tulips. Evelyn's Story

Lost in Time

Evelyn looked at her mobile. Jean was calling. She hit the answer button, 'Hello Jean, Yes, It's Evelyn. It's me here, yes. Do you have any news? Do you know where George is?'

Jean took a breath. It was her intention to keep the issue of

'The Missing George' as alive as long as possible. She didn't want

Evelyn to lose hope, and she wanted to keep hope alive, even if George wasn't. Having attempted to make some connections from the data on Evelyn's phone Jean soon realised that George's mobile was a 'burner phone. And it was definitely flat.'

Although she rang it a couple of times with no answer, she didn't leave any messages.

'Evelyn, I was hoping to find his employer's name from the phone but no luck with the phone company. Now, it is possible that he is well out of range from a tower.'

'But Jean, it has been nearly 6 weeks since he last called. I think he may have just, well, decided that he didn't want me anymore.'

'No, I don't think that would be the case. From what I know of men, once they have committed as George has done, I think he is all for you. There is every possibility that something may have gone wrong. He is in love with you, Evelyn, I just know it.'

Jean began to feel that Evelyn may want to give up. 'When he came to stay with you, did he drive here? Can you recall a car number plate? I am worried too but I have a couple more places to visit before we go to the police.

Evelyn's brow furrowed, 'Why the police?'

'Well, I'm concerned that something may have happened to him. It would be good if you had a work name or phone number so I can follow up. Did he ever give you a business card? 'What about photos, did you ever take selfies on your mobile phone?'

'I think he took photos on his phone, but I don't think he used mine.'

'I don't remember, but I'll check. Something that I have just remembered, though, is that when he bought that teapot for me all those months ago, he gave me the receipt. I still have that. In fact, I think I left it in the pot! He used his bank card to pay, would that help.'

'Hell, yes, it certainly would. That means I can go to the bank and ask about the account. I will pretend to be Mrs Mitchell.

Would you give me, say, 50 or something to bank into the account, then I'll ask the teller for the receipt and statement, which should have his details on it. Well done, Evelyn. We are on to something here and I'll certainly help you to sort this out.'

Evelyn handed Jean the $50 giving her the chance to leave Evelyn at home as she headed out to the bank.

'I'll get back to you as soon as I have the account details,' said Jean as she quickly climbed into her car.

The Bank Account

Jean parked and headed into George's bank. Waiting in line she took some deep breaths and relaxed so she could be cool and calm at the counter. Her turn came soon.

'Hello, I'm Mrs Mitchell, I just want to bank £50 into this account, please, and can I get a statement, too? Thank you.' Jean smiled.

They call them Customer Service Officers now but to her, they were still Tellers. The young lady turned to her computer and clicked on a few keys. With a slightly furrowed brow, she turned to Jean.

'I'm sorry, Mrs Mitchell, but this account has been closed. Was there another one you could use?'

'What do you mean closed?' Jean took a breath. Reaching for the paper receipt and the £50, Jean let out a throaty, gruff sound and scowled.

'Typical man. He's given me the wrong account number. I'll come back later. Thank you.'

Jean turned around quickly and hurried out of the bank, walking towards her car.

Damn, how could that have happened, she wondered? That's odd. Why did Carol close the account? Now, the trail may go cold. Can't let Evelyn know. I'll tell her that the bank will message me with the details. That will give me a couple of days.

Jean realised that she was running out of ideas on how to keep Evelyn involved before she really felt that George had left her. But maybe, just maybe, she could push the idea of going to the police and reporting a 'Missing Man.' Maybe she would go to the police on her own and give some details about George. Well, at least she knew where he lived after all.

Jean sat and thought for a moment. She needed to catch up with Carol soon anyway. How can she pull this together to make it work? Perhaps if I go to the police with Evelyn, describe George and see if the police follow up with Carol. Perhaps if they realise that

George was having an affair, then they may think that Carol did kill George all because of the affair.

Jean headed back to Evelyn, thinking as she drove about the next steps. She pulled up near Evelyn's house as her phone rang.

'Hello, this is Jean.'

'Jean, this is Carol. I need to speak to you as soon as possible. When do you think you could get here to my house?' Jean thought quickly.

'Give me a couple of hours. I have a short call to make, and then I'll head over. See you soon.' Jean hung up.

She sat back in the car seat. Things were moving a bit too quickly.

Carol's phone rang. 'Hello, this is Carol Mitchell.'

'Mrs Mitchell, Hello, this is Frances Brown from your bank. Sorry that we haven't seen you for a while but I was just wondering, did you call in recently to deposit some funds into your old personal account?'

'No, Frances, I closed an account some while ago. I don't know anybody who would deposit funds into that account unless it was somebody from Mr Hunter's office. He's my solicitor, but he would know which account to use. I would have given him the new account number. If you look at my accounts, you will see another one with a much larger balance. Thank you for the call.' Frances hung up. Turning to her fellow Customer Service Officer. She commented, 'That's odd. You are right, though. That wasn't Mrs Mitchell at all. She said that she didn't come in and she knew that the account was closed. I think that I had better report this to Customer Security.'

Chapter 6

Dr. Angela's Story

Fully Focused

Angela took Carol by the arm and helped her stand and get on her feet. She seemed to have recovered from her 'little turn.'

Angela could not remember a focus group member ever having such a reaction to the questions. This interested her.

The depth of the questions really seemed to expose some underlying issues in Carol's life. Perhaps she needed some 'closer support.' Something that Angela felt she would like to consider providing.

As Carol agreed to let Angela take her home, Angela felt that there might be a mutual feeling and perhaps an opportunity to pursue things a bit further. Angela felt rather excited at the thought of a relationship with Carol. Infact, she realised that she couldn't take her eyes off her during the whole time that the focus group was working. This felt like much more than 'the close friendships' she had experienced before when she was an undergrad.

Closing up the room Angela walked with Carol down to her car. 'Carol, look, it may be safer if I drive you home. I'm happy to stay the night if that is OK, and we can come back for your car tomorrow. Would that suit you?'

Carol glanced at Angela. 'Yes, that would be very helpful, Thank You.'

Carol felt really odd. She had never had a lesbian relationship before, but right now, it seemed that this would be the perfect way to get George out of her sexual life altogether. She couldn't help hoping that this meeting may just lead to something more…. She didn't really know where or what, but she had been in a similar position before. Although that didn't seem like a lesbian relationship. Oh God, the family secrets are bubbling to the surface. She just wanted to feel Angela's hands on her body, the gentle touch of a woman reminded her of her childhood. On the drive home, she turned to glance at Angela. She saw her beautiful soft looking lips, elegant hands, and slender neck. God, I want her tonight, she thought.

Angela's heart was racing. Her pulse is pumping with anticipation of what may be. Would Carol surrender to her advances and sleep with her tonight? It was only a short drive, and pretty soon, Angela pulled up where Carol suggested.

'Come on in. Would you like a coffee or a tea? Sorry, I don't have any wine. George, my now-deceased husband, never let me drink alcohol.'

'Tea would be nice. Thanks. By the way, which room would you like me to sleep in?'

Carol turned to look at Angela. For the first time in her life she realised that the thought of a mutual relationship was burning in her body. It was instant.

Carol took another step towards Angela. Reaching for Angela's hand she looked her in the eyes. 'My bed. Sleep with me tonight, I want you any way I can have you. Have me and make love to me.'

Angela threw her arms around Carol, kissing her on the lips with a passion that Carol had not felt for so many years. They held each other tightly, feeling like their urges would burst through their bodies.

Carol would never be able to describe how beautiful that moment felt. For the first time in her adult life, she felt truly wanted.

She knew that their passion would carry them beyond their wildest dreams. The touch of Angela's hands on her face went beyond any feelings she had experienced since she was a child on the farm. One day, she would share her childhood secrets with Angela, but right now, she just wanted to feel Angela naked and in bed with her. Carol held Angela's hand and took her upstairs.

In the early morning light, Carol looked at Angela. They smiled and Carol gently touched Angela on her lips. 'Don't say anything. I think we both feel that our lives have changed.

Happiness is there before us. I want you more than I ever realised. We can talk later, but in the meantime …… kiss me and touch me all over my body, then let me make you breakfast.'

Angela realised that today was the first day of a new life for both of them. 'That sounds rather lovely. Thank you. Black tea, no sugar.' They smiled at each other as Carol turned and went down to the kitchen.

Chapter 7

The Mirrors Reflection. Carol's Story.

Love's Tale

Angela and Carol sat together, eating breakfast. Few words were spoken, but the smiles on each face said it all. Carol reached out to touch Angela's hand. 'Thank you for being with me last night. I am afraid to ask, but will you want to see me again?'

Angela's heart gave a sudden pump. 'Every moment that we can be together will be the moment that I want to be with you. I want to share time with you. I want to make love to you so you can have the pleasures that you told me you have missed all these years. Trust me, Carol, and take me to your heart. I want you.'

Carol felt elated. How can this lady make me feel this way? Has my life been so messed up just because I could never understand my own true feelings? My life as a child on the farm was so screwed up, the way I was treated, what they did to me. There is no feeling of forgiveness that I can ever deliver to those bastards.

Carol let her happiness shine through as she stood up to just cuddle Angela. This feeling is so wonderful, she thought to herself.

Angela looked up at Carol.

'I hate to say this but I have to go now, work calls and I need to take a tutorial. An Associate professor's life is always a busy one. I will call you tonight provided that I don't have any other meetings. I want to see you again tonight and sleep with you.'

The Chatter Arrives Again

The bed was made, and the breakfast cups and plates all washed up and put away. Carol was ready to talk to Jean. She was not quite sure how to discuss things, but Jean had put her at ease the last time so it should be easy.

The knock on the door let Carol know that Jean had arrived. 'Hello, come on in. Lovely to see you again. Would you like a tea or a coffee?'

'Black tea, please.' Jean noticed the total change in Carol's demeanour. Compared to the first meeting, Carol seemed like a whole new person. She didn't even ask her to take off her shoes at the door. Infact, she didn't even ask at all and plus Jean noticed that Carol was walking around with her shoes on. What's happened, she wondered.

'Jean, when we first met, I was trying to get over my husband's accidental death. I think I told you that he fell down the stairs, but perhaps what I didn't tell you was that ….,' she hesitated, deciding that she wouldn't tell the truth of the push, but rather tell of his behaviour towards her.

'Jean, he was such an utter narcissist and bully. He lied to me about his work. He said he was a civil engineer, but he wasn't. He said he had to go away on work trips, and he started to go away for 4 weeks at a time, sometimes longer. I never knew where he went, but he said it was for work. It didn't do to ask him because he would just get into such a foul temper. I actually think he was probably having an affair, but I didn't care, at least he left me alone. I feel sorry for the poor woman that he may have met.'

Jean didn't flinch but she did squeeze her toes together. Well that answers a whole raft of questions, she thought. What will I tell Evelyn? I will obviously have to tell her something otherwise, the poor lady will go nuts. But what would happen?

So George was having an affair with Evelyn, but poor Evelyn had no idea. She thought that George was a widower……Of course, he would say anything. Do I tell Carol about the affair that George was having with Evelyn or did she know about it so she murdered George by pushing him down the stairs? Jeepers creepers, this is going to get messy. The questions swirled around in Jean's mind, but no answers were forthcoming.

'And then Jean,' continued Carol, 'the strangest thing happened recently. My bank rang to tell me that a lady went in and tried to deposit some money into my old, closed account, telling them that she was me. When they told her that the account was closed, she grabbed the money and what looked like a receipt and left the branch. I'm just afraid that someone might be trying to get at my money. George left quite a lot. I'll talk to the bank later about security. But there is some good news……. I've met someone, a lady.'

'She is an Assoc professor at the Uni. I'm really excited. I've never felt so happy since I left the farm, and I think this could become a loving relationship.'

Jean began to feel as if she was on a helter-skelter ride at the fairground. She had to ask, 'What does she teach at Uni?' Carol sat back in the chair with a look of happiness on her face.

'Well I met her when she was conducting a focus group last week. She is doing research for a report on The Effects of Family Breakdowns. It seemed I qualified now that George had died!! Her full title is Associate Professor Dr Angela Groves, and she is a sociologist.'

Jean wondered if Carol could see the blood drain from her face because that is certainly how she felt right now. Amongst a few other things, Angela was one of her orphanage's best supporters. Jean couldn't believe her luck. The orphanage, she thought, I'll introduce it now and sign up Carol. Then she stopped, realising that if she mentioned the orphanage to Carol, then no doubt Carol would tell Angela and ……. She stopped ……. thinking for a moment when she heard Carol say, 'And then the police rang me too as a follow-up for a mental or emotional check.

I think it's just to see how I am going.'

'Carol, what actually happened to George? The police don't just do a follow-up to see how you are going! They must have something to discuss with you.' At this moment Jean was very relieved that she and Evelyn had not gone to the police.

'I don't know Jean. Sergeant Williams rang and left a message saying that he wanted to call in to see me and see how I was going. He interviewed me on the day George died, and I told him everything that I could, and he spoke to me again after at the inquest. It seemed quite simple, really. We had got up; I went down to the kitchen to make breakfast for George as I always did. The next thing that I heard was George calling out as he fell. I think the problem was that he used to wear old baggy pants around the house and I suspect that he tripped on the trouser bottoms. I'll call Sgt Williams back today. The problem is that if I tell the police that George was a narcissist, they may think that I pushed him down the stairs. But I didn't, Jean, I didn't!!'

'So tell me about the new lady in your life. How often have you seen her?'

'A couple of times, but enough for us to know that we can be good for each other. Why do you ask, are you envious? Well, what about you, Jean, do you have a man or perhaps a lady in your life?' Jean wasn't used to talking about herself. She liked to keep her private life exactly that, private. She needed to change the topic.'

What had come over Carol? Jean knew. Most definitely the newly found and suddenly amazing sex with Angela. Probably was. Jean could certainly remember how Angela would do that to you, how she would make you feel. Oh Yes... she could certainly remember those days when they were together. How they felt, the pleasures that they shared, the weekends in bed, laughing and kissing after Uni. Oh her kisses. Jean was beginning to feel a mix of anger and sorrow and a bit of sexual frustration …. but she had to break up with Angela she couldn't take the continuous …... Oh forget it, she mumbled to herself. Thank God it's over.

'Carol, I need to be on my way. I have a long drive to my next meeting. Thank you for the tea and it's good to see you so happy. Hope things go well with Sgt. Williams. Let me know.' Carol saw her out and waved Goodbye. The hours were ticking past. Angela would, hopefully, arrive soon.

Chapter 8

The Tulips. Evelyn's Story

Petals in the Wind

Evelyn sat beneath the old oak tree where she and George had sat many times before, enjoying a cup of tea. Her eyelids gently closed as she remembered in her mind's eye those magical moments with George, where is he? Why did he just leave me without a word of explanation? He just didn't seem to be that kind of a man.

The thought of what had happened, what he had done, made her feel so foolish. How could she just have let herself be treated in this way. Why did Jean suggest not to go to the police? It was almost as if she knew something, or is she just trying to protect me as well?

The thoughts about all of the good things that she may have lost plagued her. George had suggested so many wonderful plans, trips that they could take, wonderful gardens that they could explore and now that seemed to be all gone like a tulip petal blowing in the wind.

As she slowly began to fall asleep, she thought about Michael. All those years that they had spent together and the wonderful times they had shared. Those passionate mornings, how he would care for her, look to her needs. She could almost feel his hands on her. Thank heavens he can't see me now, she thought. He would surely tell me what a silly lady I had been.

Suddenly, like a bolt out of the blue, Evelyn opened her eyes. 'Oh good heavens.' It was one of those involuntary responses to those quiet thoughts. Suddenly, she had a wild recollection. 'Michael's cousin is in the local police force!!'

She jumped up from her chair and ran inside the house. 'Now, where the heck is his number?' Grabbing her mobile phone, she began scrolling through the contacts list.

'Graham Williams, Graham Williams, Graham Williams…. where are you?' It was like some salutary chant, lifting her spirits from sadness to absolute happiness, a total change in her emotions.

'Of course, I'll call him and ask for his advice.' In the ecstasy of that moment, she called out, 'Oh Michael, oh thank you, thank you, thank you, my sweet man.'

Finding George

Finding Graham's number, she called straight away without a second thought. Full of excitement, almost feeling as if she had won the Pools. She waited as his mobile phone rang. 'Hello, this is Graham Williams, how can I help?'

Evelyn took a deep breath. The last thing she wanted to do was rattle on like a woman possessed. She began to speak as calmly as possible.

'Hello Graham, this is Evelyn.'

'Oh Evelyn, hello. Look, I am sorry that we haven't caught up for a while but … well you know what it is like. The naughty people just don't stop.'

'That's OK, I do understand how busy you can get. I do have a reason for calling you, though. Let me just give you a brief outline and you can tell me if you think, although maybe you shouldn't tell me that I am just a silly old woman.

So here is the issue. Some months ago, I met a man here in High Laver. It's the village where I live. He was selecting tulips.

Well, we started talking about tulips, and it sort of grew from there. We got along really well and our relationship seemed to be blossoming too. I didn't see him constantly because, in his job as a civil engineer, he travelled away on contracts and could be gone for 4 weeks or so at a time. Then he would return, and we would spend time together.

Despite all of this I didn't ever get all of his work details or contacts, it just never occurred to me mainly because he would ring me from some distant place where internet or phone connections were not very good. So things were going along really well, and to be honest, I really didn't think that our relationship would develop into anything. But it did.

Then, out of the blue, he just stopped contacting me, and I haven't heard from him since. I can't believe that he would treat me like that. The last contact seems like it was probably a couple of months or more. He did tell me that he had put me down as a contact at his work, and in the event that something happened to him, his employer would contact me, but his work has not called me. My friend has been trying to work out who he is or where he might have gone. Am I just being stupid or what?'

'Well let's see, Evelyn. You don't have any contact details but presumably, you do have his name. I don't mean to sound supercilious, but I suppose that is at least a good starting point!'

'Oh yes, of course I know his name, it's George Mitchell.'

Graham took a step towards his desk and sat down in his chair. For a moment, he just couldn't believe what he had heard! A George Mitchell who loved tulips. There can't be too many of those. Graham tried to stay a bit gentle.

'Evelyn, I assume that he did have a car?' 'Oh yes, it was a green one but I couldn't tell you what it was. I'm not really a car person but I can tell you that he really liked tulips though. As I said, that was how we met. Buying tulips at the local markets here, and do you know he loved collecting teapots? He actually bought one for me.'

Graham couldn't believe what he was hearing. All of his policing instincts were pounding in his chest. His mind was racing. I'm bloody sure that he didn't just fall down the stairs, she must have pushed him.

'Evelyn, look, I have to go but let's catch up soon so we can explore this a bit further. So until we can talk again, if you remember anything else, please ring me and let me know. In the meantime, I'll try to check out any missing people reports or perhaps stolen or lost green cars. Talk soon and no you are definitely not a silly old woman by any means. By the way, it may be best not to discuss our talk with your friend. If she should ask, just tell her that you think the police are investigating another avenue, but you don't know what.

'Thank you for calling. We will talk soon.'

Graham sat back in his chair and let out a long sigh. Well, I'll be damned, he thought to himself. The strangest things that happen when you least expect them to happen. Graham turned around and spoke to his partner.

'Ken, get your coat, we have a visit to make. I'll explain on the way.' As they drove towards Carol's place, Graham outlined the conversation that he had just had with Evelyn.

'Ken, I want you to take note of the tulips in the garden and see if you can count how many teapots are in the house. If she asks why you are looking at the tulips, just tell her that they are your favourite plants and write down exactly what she says. I'm going to ask her who liked the tulips, write that answer too.'

Ken nodded. He knew Graham well, so well that he knew not to ask what this was all about. Graham would reveal all on the journey back to the station anyway.

Graham turned into Carol's street, pulling up outside of her house. He could see that Carol was at home so he walked up to the door and knocked.

The door was opened by a rather happy-looking Carol, somewhat happier than the last time Graham had spoken to her.

'Hello, Mrs. Mitchell, Sergeant Williams. Sorry for the intrusion, but we were driving by and thought we should stop by to see how things were going for you. May we come in?'

'Of course, yes, of course, please come in.' Carol felt uneasy, but she had expected this to happen at some point, which is why she never returned the call from Sgt Williams in the first place.

Sergeant Williams started the introduction. 'Mrs. Mitchell, this is Snr Constable Price. We like to follow up with families or individuals after traumatic events such as yours to ensure that you are coping with what we call Life Matters. Our experience is that you may suffer feelings such as sadness, anxiety, confusion and even exhaustion. Do you feel that you are suffering any of those feelings.? Infact, how are you feeling because you seem to be well-adjusted to life already? I notice that the teapots have gone too. Did they belong to George?'

'Oh yes, I never liked them anyway. That was George's hobby, not mine. He was always collecting them. I gave them to the 2nd Hand Shop nearby. They were very pleased to get them.'

'I noticed that all the lovely tulips have gone. Were they George's pride and joy too?'

'Him and his bloody tulips, yes, they were his.'

'The thing is, Sergeant, that when George died, I realised that I had to make a total change in my life. You can probably recognise that I am not wearing black. He never liked me to wear anything coloured so after he died, I threw out all of my black clothes and bought clothes that I liked. My styles, my colours, my choices. Frankly, I'm glad that he died. It was his own fault for wearing those bloody stupid pants. I knew he would fall one day, just not down the stairs.'

'Did you see him fall?' 'No. I think I told you before I was in the kitchen making him his breakfast. It was a frightening shout.'

'One final question, if I may. Do you know if George may have been having a relationship with anybody in a nearby village?'

'What makes you ask that?'

'Well, it's just that we had a report of a missing male called George Mitchell, who was a lover of tulips and a collector of teapots. Obviously, the report wasn't from you. It just seems strange that the report was of a man who could be George. So, if you do think of anything would you please let me know.'

Sergeant Williams handed her his card. 'We should go now and let you get on with your day. Oh, by the way, did George drive a green car?'

'Yes, he did, it's in the garage, but I can drive it now. I'm lucky to have got my licence before we got married because he wouldn't have let me drive otherwise.'

'Thank you for talking to us and take care. If there is anything we can do to help, please contact us. The number is on the card.'

Graham and Ken turned towards the front door when Carol walked towards them and said, 'Well if it was George, she is bloody lucky that he is dead and as far as I am concerned you can tell her that he is dead. He was a bastard of a man.'

'I didn't say it was she Mrs Mitchell.'

Graham and Ken got into the squad car and headed back to the police station. Sergeant Graham Williams turned to Ken. 'Well, after that little conversation, there is no doubt in my mind that Evelyn's missing partner was certainly George. Now I have two problems. The first one is to work out how to break the news to Evelyn, and the second problem is to work out whether or not George's death was accidental or on purpose. My instinct tells me that it was on purpose. However, are there some extenuating circumstances? I wonder if we are dealing with a DV case here. From some of the things that she said, I suspect that he may have been a narcissistic type. Typical signs, what she can wear, not letting her out. This may have been a most fortunate accident for Mrs Carol Mifchell.'

'Sarge, why did you make that comment? I didn't say it was a she?'

'Well, that may help her think, throw a bit of confusion into her mind!'

Back at the station Ken went and picked up the George Mitchell file to familiarise himself a bit more with the case. Maybe a deeper read of the police pathologist report would be a good place to start, he thought, followed by a chat with the police psychologist regarding narcissistic tendencies.

Chapter 9
The Chatter's Story

Lizbeth [Lizzie] Hurley

A Strange Referral

Jean sat and pondered. Had she got herself too caught up in her client's lives or was it that they needed her as a sort of sounding board or for emotional support? Either way, she didn't really care as long as they paid her fees and, where possible, supported the orphanage. There was still an opportunity to present Carol with the chance to donate to the orphanage. After all…Carol's newfound friend, Angela, was already a major donor. Perhaps she could build a bit of a challenge to see who could donate the most. Carol must have inherited a decent sum from George's death. Perhaps a visit to Carol was called for.

A New Referral.

Jean's mobile rang. She looked at the caller ID. It was her contact and referral source, Lizbeth Hurley, or Lizzie to her friends. Jean answered the call. 'Hello, My Dear, lovely to hear from you. How are you Lizzie? It's been a while since we had a chat.'

'Indeed, it has been a while, my good friend Jean. Remember I mentioned that I may have a new client for you. Well, it's a definite now. I need to meet with you for a chat. It's a male, so I need to go over the background with you.'

Lizbeth Hurley Prologue

Jean had known Lizzie for a long time. Lizzie had grown up in a rather tumultuous household where secrets and lies were commonplace. Her father was a charismatic man but untrustworthy, and her mother struggled with mental health issues. Between the two parents the home environment fostered a keen sense for uncovering the truth.

Consequently, she had revelled at Uni, where she studied Criminal Justice with a minor in Behavioural Psychology. She left Uni well-equipped with the skills to understand social dynamics. Dr Angela was indeed a great source of inspiration.

Lizzie was one of those girls with a striking appearance. Deep green eyes that would pierce right through you. She made constant changes to her hair, often putting in streaks of colours but always curly. She had the odd habit of playing with the curls as she was talking to you. Jean often wondered if it was a habit or just a way to distract you, catch you out if you weren't telling the truth or even paying attention to the conversation.

Jean remembered the sad story about the loss of Lizzie's sister Mia. When Mia died Lizzy became relentless in her pursuit of how it happened. Mia's body was found close to a stream near their home. Although still at Uni, Lizzy was ploughing her way through the evidence that she could elicit from the newspapers and monthly magazine articles.

Read all about it …Mia dead in the Mud. God, how she hated those papers.

After Uni, Lizzie decided to focus on building an internet business in Workplace Psychology, she ran some YouTube online courses about 'Social Dynamics in the Workplace.'

Consequently, she developed a number of corporate clients who used her services to monitor key clients and key staff members. Yes, it may have been spying or a breach of something or other, but these clients worked in very specific areas.

Jean had known Lizzie from their Uni days, so she agreed to come along as a support to her business. She worked with Lizzie as a sort of part-time investigator, monitoring Lizzie's clients and their individuals and providing Chat services.

Jean had always wondered about Mia's death. It had become a major media story, Journalists were everywhere, asking questions, writing stories. But when she met Carol, she realised that there may have been some family secrets pointing towards Mia that Carol would not open up about… Not yet, anyway.

Jean hypothesised that Mia may have died close to the farm that Carol had grown up on. Although she had not as yet contacted Lizzie to share any clues or her personal thoughts mainly because she worked hard to keep her client's information secret and confidential. Plus, Carol had not yet talked in any detail about the brother in the Army or, for that matter, just what the family secrets really were.

Lizzie suggested a time and place to meet which suited Jean. They hung up.

Jean finished the call and found herself pondering again. She couldn't help thinking about the new relationship that Carol had started with Angela. She couldn't blame Carol. She knew how it all went. Both Angela and Carol were single. Although Carol had been married, it was a disaster, so the attraction was understandable. She wouldn't trust a man again.

Carol was lonely and still had her personal sexual needs, and much the same for Angela. However, it made her begin to realise that maybe she felt a sense of loss or maybe a bit of envy. Her relationship with Angela had been very intense. Jean realised that she had never really experienced such a wonderful, loving time. It was the closest feeling to being in love that she had known.

She realised that she had missed their intimacy.

Chapter 10

Lizbeth [Lizzie] Hurley

Referral of Glen Spicer

The day for the meeting with Lizzie had arrived. Jean sat waiting, wondering just who this new referral may be. Lizzie had never had to discuss the person before. She normally just said here's the name, number and address; the rest is up to you, good Luck. Most times she would just email the details. Jean assumed that this must be an interesting person or else a really troubled soul. This time, it was obviously a little different.

Lizzie walked up, pulled the chair out and sat down. Green streaks in her curly hair. Different, I suppose. 'Hello, my dear, so how has life been in the Chatter's world?'

'Interesting, to say the least. A new client is proving to be very interesting. She started out as a rather staid but, I suspect, troubled lady. When I first met her, I would have thought that she had spent her life in jail. Very reserved, almost reluctant to talk. But you know me… after a while, she began to open up, and then out it all came. I just used the old 'Tell me about your husband' approach. As you have always said…. That's 95% of the problems. And blow me down, would you believe it, …… he had died in a tragic fall down the stairs. Tripped and fell, she said…. She was in the kitchen making breakfast. … Ha Ha…. What a joke…but the Coroner declared Accidental death, and so she is free. And now… guess who she has met? Angela bloody Groves.'

'Steady Jean… you left her, you know!' 'I know, it's just that I miss it! All the signs are there but Carol doesn't know of my previous connection with Angela. That bugs me because I have to be careful about getting her to support the orphanage. So, who is this new client? I'll get the coffee. Usual?'

Jean returned to the table to discuss the client. 'Tell me who and why the secrecy?'

'Jean, I've copied my notes for you rather than talk it through with you. You'll see he's a complex character. Joined the Army and showed promise, but his RSM [Regimental Sergeant Major] noticed a few issues and took steps to interview him and eventually had him psych tested. Anyway, the notes tell it all. The thing is that he grew up near where Mia died. So be careful, protect yourself, you understand? Not saying that he did it but there is nothing to say that he wasn't involved. You may remember that she was raped too. What sort of person rapes a 14-year-old girl???'

'Wow, this one needs to be treated carefully then.'

'Spot on Jean, spot on.'

Jean was about to discuss Carol but thought better of it and said nothing. Carol had originally been referred to by Jean's contact at the local social welfare association. Her contact worked at the Magistrates Court and would sometimes refer people to Jean from there, so it was unlikely that Lizzie knew anything about Carol being Jean's client.

'Let me read your notes and I'll follow him up. I assume his contact number is in the notes. Thank you for the business. Did you happen to mention any fee structure to him or does he know nothing about me as yet?'

'I just told him that someone will call him and arrange to meet him. I knew you would be happy with a new client so it is up to you regarding costs. Maybe he will support the orphanage, too. By the way, here's his contact details. At least I got the phone number and address.'

'I won't ask you how, but thanks again, Lizzie. I'll report back regarding any clues.'

Jean reached out and shook hands with Lizzie, smiled and walked towards her car. Lizzie went in to buy another coffee.

Chapter 11

The Tulips. Evelyn's Story

Tulips turning Brown

Evelyn went back to her chair under the tree for a while. Well, at least Graham hadn't laughed at me when we were talking, she thought. He even sounded serious for a moment. Hope he comes up with some news eventually.

Before I head up to bed, I might even make a cup of tea in George's teapot. Turning on the kettle, she reached for the teapot to put the leaves in. 'Yes, I know, George, I should heat the pot first, but I just want a cuppa.' She lifted the little lid, 'That's funny, where has the receipt gone?' She said to nobody in particular. Jean had it last, but why didn't she give it back to me?

Darkness was closing in when the phone rang. It was Graham. 'Hi Evelyn, how has the day been? Sorry to call you a bit latish, but I wanted to head over before you settled in for the night. Is it too late to call in?'

'Of course not. Infact, I have just put the kettle on so I can reheat it when you arrive. See you soon.'

'Hope that is good, thought Graham, she sounds quite OK. Perhaps after all this time she has come to terms with the probable loss of George. Well, let's see how she is after I tell her that George is dead.

Arriving at Evelyn's house, Graham parked and walked up the path, stopped at the front door and knocked gently. 'Evelyn …. it's Graham.' Evelyn opened the door smiling. 'Happy to see you.

Come on in, kettle is boiling.'

Graham followed Evelyn into the kitchen and sat at the table. No point in putting off the talk, he thought. 'Evelyn, I have found out about George and the car. The news is not good, so you may want to sit down. It may all be a bit confusing, so I think it is best if I start at a point well before you both met.'

Graham waited for Evelyn to finish making a cup of tea. In a slow but precise way, Graham told Evelyn about George. His marriage to Carol, his odd ways, the possibility that he was a narcissist, the lies about his work and the reasons he was constantly away. Finally, his untimely death falling down the stairs. How the Coroner declared it an Accidental Death in that he tripped and fell.

Graham made sure that he didn't confuse the discussion by adding any of his own private views as to what he felt really happened, namely that Carol had pushed him. That's a police investigation matter, he assured himself.

'So you see, he didn't just stop seeing you, he had infact died. Maybe in the long run, it was a mixed blessing for you. When people like George meet a new woman or at least a woman who may seem an ideal partner, they will go all out to win that person's affection and almost 'love bomb' them to show how wonderful they are. It may have appeared that he was the perfect person at the start, but it quickly changed. He may have changed, but unfortunately, characters like George don't really change. Are you OK, Evelyn?'

'Yes Graham, I'm fine. I was just thinking back to my marriage with Michael. He was truly a beautiful man to me in every way so I just cannot see how I was so stupid to fall for George as I did.'

'Evelyn, you were not stupid at all. You had been alone for some years, and then you met George. His approach to you would have been totally disarming, and some victims will even say intoxicating, leading you to ignore your better judgement. So please don't blame yourself. Thank the heavens above that you were saved. The problem is that these men will mirror your emotions, so what you think is your soulmate is just a reflection of you.'

Evelyn looked up at Graham. 'I would like to see his grave if that is possible. Do you know where he is buried?'

'I'm not sure, but I will email you tomorrow. His details will be in the file. I am sorry that I was the bearer of bad news, but in a way, the outcome was a blessing for you. I hope you remember that. I need to go, so thank you for the tea and I'll email you tomorrow. Take care.'

Graham walked back to his car, feeling even more determined to solve the situation surrounding George's death.

Evelyn waved Graham farewell and turned back inside, picking up her phone as she went to contact Jean. 'It's getting late, so I'll send a message,' she murmured to herself.

The message to Jean was short and to the point. 'Hello Jean, Police have confirmed that George is dead. Getting details of gravesite. Call me tomorrow if you want more information Evelyn.'

The following morning Evelyn read her message from Graham. 'Hi, Evelyn, "St. Mary's Church, The Street, High Ongar" It's on the same side as The Foresters Arms.'

Evelyn realised that she knew exactly where it was. She often drove into Epping to do her weekly shopping so that she would have driven straight past St Mary's Church on quite a few occasions. How uncanny, she thought. Here I was, driving straight past his bloody grave and had no idea he was there. She went into her bedroom and changed.

What are you doing? She asked herself as she dressed? Evelyn looked at herself in the mirror. I lost a good man in Michael, and then I made a big mistake with George. I fell for his smooth charm. Thank heavens for the explanation that Graham gave me otherwise, I would seriously think that I am a stupid old lady.

Well, your next steps will get him well and truly out of your system, she muttered to herself. She smiled a wicked smile. She couldn't believe what she was about to do. Picking up the teapot, she wrapped it up in a plastic bag. She didn't want to spill anything.

Evelyn knew the way, so she just drove steadily. Arriving in High Ongar, she parked the car outside of the post office, picked up the bag and crossed the road to walk through the lychgate into the graveyard. She had to wander around for a while as she looked for George's grave. Finally, she felt a flood of relief flow through her. Found it. She unwrapped the teapot and placed it on top of the gravestone.

She was just about to empty the contents of the pot when a voice called out to her, 'Heh, what are you doing?' It was Carol but Evelyn didn't know who she was.

'Well, to be perfectly honest, lady I am about to empty this teapot of urine all over this grave! So do you know this man?'

'Do I ever. George Mitchell was my husband. I was married to the old bastard for 20 odd years. Lucky for me, he fell down the stairs and broke his neck and died right where he fell. I come here once a week to curse him. And it looks like you are about to do the same thing and probably throw a pot of piss over him too.'

Carol started laughing, and she laughed and laughed and laughed until her sides were just aching. 'Oh my god, this is wonderful, couldn't be better. Come on, you pour, and I'll curse.'

'I'll happily pour, and then I shall smash the bloody teapot on the grave.'

Carol burst out laughing again. 'Ha ha, I got rid of my teapots too…..'

And so, between the both of them they jointly carried out their emotional cleansing. For Carol, this would be the last time that she would need to visit the grave, and for Evelyn, she no longer felt that she was a silly old woman.

After the cleansing ceremony was over they stood silently side by side neither realising who they were and how close they were to each other. If Jean could see them now, she would probably have a fit.

Carol broke the silence. 'He hurt you, didn't he? He certainly hurt me for nearly 22 years. You are just so lucky that I killed him.'

'What do you mean you killed him?'

'Well, I didn't actually kill him, I just pushed him down the stairs. I didn't mean to, it just happened. Before I knew what happened I realised that I pushed him. Let's go to the Forester Arms for a drink.'

'Just a mo. I'm going to send my Chatter a message.' Evelyn reached for her phone and typed a message to Jean. "Hi, have found George's grave and cleansed myself of his memory. Met his wife Carol, too. We are now both cleansed of his memory. What a wonderful feeling. Off to The Foresters Arms for a celebration drink with Carol. Catch up soon. Evelyn."

Chapter 12

The Chatter's Story

All Good Things

Jean found herself trying to pull the threads of the past two days together. Although happy to have received another referral from Lizzie and having read the notes on the Spicer family, she was nonetheless somewhat uneasy about the nature of the person or persons concerned.

She had initially felt uneasy as she listened to Carol discuss her early days on the farm and yet, at the same time be a bit vague about her brother and her father. Jean had never heard his name mentioned, but with the same surname, it was blatantly obvious that the two were related.

Two things she urgently needed to do. First, establish if Glen was the brother who went off to the army, and second, check on Carol's maiden name. Was she really Carol Spicer or had she perhaps been adopted or what the hell is the situation?

Jean wondered if she should at least open up to Lizzie about her contact with Carol, but she just wasn't sure. She thought it best to first work out her strategy before taking any further steps. Besides, she hadn't really gathered much information about Carol's background other than since her marriage to George.

The light on her phone indicated that there were some messages. Better check, she thought, as she picked up the phone and hit the messages button. Ah, a message from Evelyn. What's up with her now? …. Jean stared at the message. The words 'Police advise, George Dead' had previously burned into her eyes, and now it was 'Have found George's grave.' it was all she could do to blink and stare at the message.

A feeling of numbness spread all over her. Her blood ran cold. She sat down. How in the hell had Evelyn been able to discover that George was dead? And then she thought, how had the police been able to link Evelyn to George.

Jean was trying to clear her head, thinking about all the possible connections. She had worked really hard to keep each client's details a secret and keep them apart.

The fact that Evelyn had managed to discover these connections was just what she didn't want to happen.

Evelyn doesn't even know about Carol, well at least I don't think so, Jean thought, slowly trying to imagine if it was even possible. They don't even live near each other. What's going to happen if Carol and Evelyn meet. She tried to imagine the scenario. They were two very different women. Carol, a lady who had suffered years of domestic violence from a totally narcissistic husband and she, was now about to become involved with Angela in a lesbian relationship. Evelyn, who had enjoyed a beautiful, loving relationship with her husband Michael, would now discover a side of life that she may have never experienced. At least, I don't think so, she thought.

Jean's phone peeped, another message coming in. 'Hi, Have found George's grave and cleansed me of his memory. Met his widowed wife, Carol too. We are now cleansed of his memory.

What a wonderful feeling. Tell more later. Off to The Foresters Arms for a celebration drink with Carol. Catch up soon. Evelyn.'

This was all a bit too much. Jean felt as if she was going to faint. She thought she should get a coffee now. First, Carol meets Angela, then Lizzie's referral and now Evelyn is learning about George and meeting Carol. This is all becoming a bit too much, she thought, what's happening?

I just don't want all good things to come to an end.

Jean realised that she had to get her head straight. She started to recite the Power Acronym that she used when things got on top of her. ACED, ACED, ACED……. Aware, Control, Expect, Decide; Aware, Control, Expect, Decide, she chanted.

She knew that she had to be Aware of the situation, get Control of her emotions and fears, expect things to change, don't worry and Decide what outcome she wanted.

Good old Angela. She taught me so many good ways to just be in control of myself.

She got up to make a coffee.

Chapter 13

Lizbeth 'Lizzie' Hurley

Memories of Mia

It had been a long time since Lizzie had spoken to Jean, but she needed to catch up and fill her in on the Mia investigation to date, as well as put some plans into place with Jean. After all the years that had gone by, Lizzie was never going to allow Mia's memory to fade.

A gentle and caring 14-year-old girl doing no harm to anyone is brutally raped and murdered, then left in the mud on the river bank. Lizzie had made a promise to Mia on the day that she was buried that she would leave no stone unturned to discover who killed her. Who in the hell would do such a thing?

Those sessions that she had with Angela helped to keep her on track. Helped her to focus on the task at hand. Despite having to run her own business she put all her spare time into trying to discover who killed Mia.

Lizzie had worked tirelessly to investigate and eliminate the many suspects that she had identified. Slowly, slowly, she knew that she would find Mia's killer or killers. Sadly, the case had gone cold but the investigating police had never given up. After each 3 years, they would reopen the now cold case, having tested any new forensic evidence that they may have uncovered. Just like Lizzie, they were determined to find the guilty party.

Lizzie felt that it was time to bring in Jean, her trusted Chatter, to work with her on what she was convinced was a very strong lead.

Jean was having a sip of her coffee when a sudden notification on her mobile beeped. She put Lizzie's notes down and reached for the phone. A message from Lizzie. 'Hi, can we meet at KG Coffee shop in Chipping Ongar? The normal coffee shop?

Want to run over the notes with you. Say 3 pm.'

She got up to wash her face and set off for Chipping Ongar. What's all this going to be about, she wondered.

Having gone over the notes from Lizzie, it was plain to see that she was devastated by Mia's death, and Jean suspected that the constant searching and investigating on her own, trying to uncover what really happened, was taking its toll.

From the notes it seems that Lizzie had discovered that there was a family friendship between Mia and the Spicer family. Something that Jean had not discovered yet. A family connection that she didn't know existed. So it would seem likely that Glen Spicer who had left the village to go into the army, was Carol's older brother. So, was it possible that there had been a friendship between Glen and Mia?

Lizzie was on her way over to meet with Jean, unaware of the fact that Jean had a connection with the lady who would have been Carol Spicer and, therefore, Glen Spicer's younger sister.

Jean sat waiting for Lizzie feeling a bit nervous because right now she realised that she had never told Lizzie about her relatively new connection with Carol. Well, it was never an issue and to date, there had only been two meetings with Carol, and both had very different outcomes.

First, there was the meeting after her husband George had died with the subsequent inquest and burial, followed by the other meeting that Carol had requested where she had a complete change of demeanour and sprouted out about the new relationship with Angela. Jean couldn't forget about the shoes. It wasn't only that though; it was the obvious happiness that Carol was exuding over the new relationship with Angela. She couldn't help it but she felt very jealous about that.

The other issue that drifted into Jean's mind was that she didn't really know anything about Carol's family either. Is it possible that Carol's father or brother may have had a dark past?

Maybe another meeting with Carol should be arranged. Jean sat and waited for Lizzie. Damn, she thought I'll call Carol now to make time.

She reached for her mobile. As she sat back to call Carol she saw Lizzie standing there, 'Who are you calling?'

Lizzie's Frustration

'For Christ's sake don't creep up on me like that. For the moment, let's just say I'm about to call Carol. She is a relatively new client that I have only seen twice. I need to catch up with her and after you and I have had our discussion, you may understand why.'

Lizzie walked into the shop, ordered two coffees, came straight out and sat at the table. 'Have you had time to read the notes I handed you? Plus, do you know anything about the Spicer family?'

'To answer that I need to go back a bit. Carol is a new client. When she was referred to me she was in the coroner's court after the death of her husband. He had fallen down the stairs, broken his neck and died at home. When I met her, she was Mrs Mitchell. Strange lady, definitely a DV victim, narcissistic husband. Basically screwed in the head. When we were talking she made strange comments about her family secrets, her brother gone to the army, that sort of thing.

I didn't press for his name. That was for later. Some mention about family secrets… but that was all. I didn't want to push her at the first meeting.

The next meeting was a couple of weeks later, and wow….. an all-new lady, house all changed, new clothes, the lot. Teapots gone, tulips pulled out. And then came the confession……. I've met a new lady…..Guess who she has met?…… You know who …..I told you before …….. Dr Angela Groves!! They are now bloody lovers. I had to get out of there straight away and arrange to go back later. So now I have read your notes and Whamooo, Carol Spicer got married to George Mitchell and is Carol Mitchell and Glen Spicer's younger sister. That's why I was calling ..…arranging my next meeting. Now, what would you like to discuss.'

'Jean, I'm sorry. I've put you in a bit of a spot. I didn't realise that you had already established a connection, however tenuous, with Carol.'

'Don't worry, I'll still go back anyway and continue my discussions as if I didn't know anything. Knowing something makes it a bit easier to steer the conversation to get some better outcomes for you.'

'So …. let me tell you what I know. The Spicers were never really considered as possible suspects. The parents denied knowing Mia, there was no sign of Glen as he had joined the army before

Mia's body was found, and there was no investigation by the police of them.'

'They lived on a small farm near Fyfield. It just so happens that the River Roding, which is where Mia was found, runs past Fyfield. I ask you, why were they not considered suspects? I think it is more than likely that Carol may have known Mia, possibly through school. But Carol was never interviewed as she was a minor.'

'At the moment, I can't get my hands on school records because that has to be a police request. I've spoken to them, but there is not sufficient to reopen the cold case.'

Chapter 14
Angela Calls In

Loves Desire

Down the hall Carol's phone rang. 'One of these days, I'm going to get a mobile she thought. 'Carol, it's me, Angela. You must be at home if you answered your phone….. ha-ha… gosh, that's so funny these days….. one day we'll get you a mobile… I'm missing you, my sweet lady. I'll be leaving the uni soon. I can't wait to be with you. I want to hold you and kiss you all over your body. I've picked up a couple of bottles of wine so that we can toast our future. Are you OK?'

'Oh God, Angela, I want you so much too and I have lots to tell you about what happened the other day. Come soon. I can't stand the wait; I want you too.'

Angela just knew that her life would change. Carol was just what she needed. A lady who had lived a somewhat troubled life and was ready to move towards happiness and pleasure. From the little that Carol had mentioned about her previous married life, she was amazed at how well-balanced she seemed to be. Even the death of her, albeit narcissistic husband, didn't seem to have affected her, if anything, she seemed to have broken free from the horrors of that relationship and was happy.

She knew that it would not take long for Carol to fall madly in love with her. Angela had experienced a relationship like this before. She always remembered Jean, deeply emotional and so ready to be loved. But Carol, well. she is a whole new thing. Naive and eager, needing to be wanted. But the way she responds to me is wonderful. She will be able to form such a healthy relationship.

But Angela knew. Her struggle with the stigma surrounding mental illness, particularly in an academic world that prizes intellect and composure, may add stress and strain to her relationship with Carol. She might be able to hide her struggles from colleagues and students, fearing judgment or loss of respect, but from Carol, it may be harder.

Whilst she saw such a balance in Carol she felt her own internal conflict. She realised that she is constantly trying to maintain an outward appearance of self-control, despite feeling chaotic inside. Maybe her eagerness to be in love with Carol will help her overcome these feelings of emotional inadequacy. Forget her troubles.

Coming Home

Angela hurried home to Carol. Parking the car in her drive she grabbed the wine and almost ran up to the front door. She was about to knock when …..Wooosh …the door flew open, and Carol was standing there with arms outstretched.

'Come to me, my Dear Lady. Kiss me upon my sweet lips, and my arms are here to hold you,

'Press hard upon my hips,'

'Heh, that is a beautiful welcome…… Give me more!'

Carol grabbed hold of Angela and kissed her gently on her lips, running her hands across her body. 'My God, I want you Angela, let's open the wine and toast to the beautiful night that awaits us. Come let me wine and dine you.'

Angela glanced at the table in the dining room. There, laid out with tablecloth and china, was a setting fit for a lover.

'Dinner is ready. Take a seat, and let me feed the inner lady.' Angela sat and watched as Carol brought out a wonderful Irish stew. 'Crickey, that looks rather delicious. Let me open the wine. A rather nice Pinot Noire, how did I know that it would go so well with our dinner.'

Angela felt the tensions of the day fall away as she sat to enjoy a beautiful dinner and a glass of wine with Carol. She knew that they both wanted to go to bed and spend the night together, but that would come soon.

Picking up her glass, she turned to look at Carol. 'But first, tell me your news.'

For a moment, Carol wondered if she should open up as much as she had done with Evelyn. Maybe not, she thought to herself, not quite yet.

'Well, you probably don't know because I haven't told you, but once a week, I call in to St Mary's Church in High Ongar. That's where George is buried. I go there to his gravesite to spend 10 minutes telling him what a bastard he was to me, etc etc. It's my way of letting go of some curses and it helps me to simply let go of my anger. I used to take a teapot and smash it on the grave but now that I have got rid of them, I don't!!'

So, for a while, it has worked for me. My anger is slowly dissipating, and I know that as my poor brain attempts to protect itself from painful memories, it won't lead to gaps in my memory regarding my childhood events, which worries me. There are some of those that I need to get rid of too but that is to tell you about later. Gosh, I hope that you don't think I may be some kind of nutcase, but it all works for me.

Well, a couple of days ago I turned up at the grave only to see another lady standing there with a teapot in her hand. It looked like she was about to pour something onto the grave, so I called out to her. Just a gentle 'What are you doing?' She looked at me and asked, 'Did you know this man? So I said Sure do, he was my husband.'

'Well, the look on her face seemed to indicate that she was a bit astounded. I walked up to her and stood next to her. She looked at me and said, 'But you can't be, he told me his wife was dead', she said in a rather slow, puzzled voice. She seemed to be such a beautiful lady. So I smiled and said, Well it's the other way around. He is now dead and I'm alive!! So I asked her what she was doing here! What she told me was quite interesting.

It turns out that she was his lover. He had told her a pack of lies about himself, just like he had told me. I felt so sorry for her when I realised that she may have fallen for his rubbish life story.

Anyway, we agreed to have a 'cleansing ceremony.' I would chant my curses as she poured a teapot of whatever it was onto the grave. It turned out to be urine!!! Can you believe that she was going to piss all over his grave!!! How hilarious. So we carried out our cleansing and decided to go to The Foresters Arms for a drink and a chat!!

She is such a nice lady. Mind you, after I had told her about George she realised how lucky she was to have 'dodged a bullet' so to speak. I told her a bit about you and me, though, hope you don't mind.'

'I don't mind at all, in fact, I am quite pleased that you feel good enough about us to want to tell somebody.'

Angela had a puzzled look on her face, 'What an amazing time you both had. Finding her at George's grave must have been a surprise for you. Did she happen to tell you how she found out where he was buried, and did she even tell you where she lived?'

Carol stopped for a moment from telling any more of the story. She certainly wasn't going to say anymore or tell what she had said about George's death. Realising that she had opened up to Evelyn way too much had made her suddenly feel cold. Oh God, what have I done? She thought to herself.

Angela started again with the questions. 'Do you know anything about Evelyn?' Carol had never felt so stupid. She just wanted to burst into tears.

'Did you tell her anything else? You haven't really told me much about George yet so what did you tell her??? Firstly, I mean did you happen to tell her how he died? If he died at home was there an autopsy and a Coroner's inquest? Did you tell her about the Coroners Court? Did she ask you about that? Did she ask how much the police are involved? Out of interest how often have they spoken to you?'

'Yes, I told her about the Coroners Court and the visits from the police. But I was very careful not to tell her too much about what I said to Sgt Graham Williams.'

'Carol, Why the hell did Sgt Graham Williams come to see you again?'

'Well, he said that it was part of the follow-up, and it is what they do to make sure that the family or the wife is coping ok with the situation.'

'Carol did you even think about what the hell was going on or was it simply that the very moment you felt you could talk to someone who had known George, it just seemed to set you free?'

Carol felt very intimidated at this point. Why was Angela being so angry with her and asking all these questions? Hell, she is treating me like a child, thought Carol.

What Carol didn't yet understand about Angela was the problem with Angela's sense of fear and vulnerability, which would start to come to the fore. She was beginning to feel her anxiety over her private life becoming public. If the whole issue about George's death was rather sordid, would people judge her over the relationship with Carol? Would the fact that she was a lesbian having a relationship with a person involved in a sordid death tarnish her professional reputation? What would that mean to her future tenure as an Assoc Prof? Talk about doing research about Family Breakdowns… What a joke.

Angela's mind was racing. She felt so aware of her possible fall into depression and anxiety. It often leads her to keep others at arm's length, so the thought of something as personal as her romantic or emotional involvement with Carol being discussed openly would feel invasive.

If it became a story in the press, how would she handle the questions, how would she avoid the looks from the student's eyes?

Her time with Jean certainly showed her that this vulnerability might make her defensive or even provoke her to withdraw as she scrambles to maintain her privacy. This is what happened as she and Jean discovered each other. Jean couldn't cope with it so they broke up.

She had to meet Jean again to talk this through. She would call tomorrow. But right now, she needed to make sort of angry love to Carol, to feel her body all over, to make love the way she wanted, deeply and very, very intently. Her need for sex was becoming overwhelming.

Chapter 15
The Chatters Story

A Call from Dr Angela Groves

Jean was expecting a call from Lizzie Hurley so as her mobile rang she didn't look to see who was calling. Much to her surprise, she heard Angela's voice.

'Jean, it's Angela, please don't hang up. I know you may want to, but I need to talk to you reasonably soon, if not sooner. When are you free, and where can we meet? I can come to Chelmsford if that fits in for you.'

'Well, Hello Angela, are you OK? You sound a bit harassed. What's up or do you need to meet to discuss?'

'I'm OK. It's just that I didn't want you to hang up. I want to see you. Talk to you face to face, you know, like humans used to do!! Are you still working as a Chatter?'

'I certainly am. Is this about your new lover? She started to tell me a bit about you two. Obviously, you haven't mentioned us yet. That's a bit hard for me to help you on that one. You should know she is a new client. You know that I still want you. I'm sure you know that.'

'It sort of is about that, but more about a situation that has arisen that may involve a client or a couple, depending on if the other one is a client. I think they may have got close and could end up causing a few problems for us both, so that is part of the reason I want to see you, plus anything else that may happen.'

'Is Witham still convenient? Yes, I know that's where you live, and I still think of you…. … The café there is nice. Anyway, send me a message if you need to check your diary, preferably after classes please.'

'Angela, who are the two people involved? Obviously, Carol is one, but who is the other?'

'All I know is that she is called Evelyn. Don't know where she lives. That's part of my problem. She discovered where George was buried. When I asked Carol how she knew and where she lived, Carol knew nothing, and after the event at the graveyard, they went off for a chat at The Foresters Arms in High Ongar, for God's sake, like newfound best friends.'

'OK I'll get back to you with a day and time. Take Care.'

Jean hung up, dropped her hands into her lap and let go a big sigh. She couldn't keep talking to Angela just in case something was spilled.

So it was Evelyn. Oh, crikey, what will I do now? Evelyn must have gone and told the police about George disappearing. So of course, whoever was working on the case would put two and two together and come up with 'George' being the common person!!

Bloody Hell, cursed Jean, more problems. Plus, I now have to chase up Glen Spicer before the police follow him up, and that is probably going to open up a can of worms. So I've got Carol and Evelyn and Glen to talk to but somehow keep them apart.

Tracking Glen

Jean opened her purse to take out Glen's contact details. She checked the mobile number and called. A few rings, and Glen answered.

'Yeah, hello, this is Glen, what do you want?'

'Hello Glen, my name is Jean, I'm a friend of your sister Carol. The reason for the call is to ask if we could catch up at some time. I think Carol will tell you that I can offer some support. I can explain my services and you may find them a valuable resource. By the way, you are more than welcome to check with Carol about how I can help.'

'I'm what they call a Chatter. I'll spend time talking with you so that I can be the one and only person that you can trust to discuss things with, and that may help. I am very private and trustworthy. Even Carol will never know what we talk about. Depending on how you feel, when is a good time to meet?'

Jean expected the pregnant pause that followed. She waited, knowing that the next to speak would be making a decision.

'OK, Jean, thank you. Right now, I am trying to find my way too. You may not know, and Carol may not tell you, but I received a medical discharge from the Army. Following a series of, perhaps I'll call them, minor personal confrontations, I was medically assessed, interviewed, and psych tested. The outcome seemed to be that I would be better off out of the Army and look to get rehabilitated. So right now, some personal help will be well accepted. So, to answer your question, yes, I am happy to meet. Where and when?'

Jean felt utterly amazed at how Glen had accepted the approach, especially after what he had probably gone through whilst in the Army.

'I'm pretty mobile, so I can come to your home or meet outside at a coffee shop or pub.'

'How about meeting at The White Hart in Witham? Would tomorrow at 12 suit you?'

'I can do that too. See you there. I'll be wearing a red jacket.'

Jean hung up and breathed a sigh of relief. She thought to herself that at least he sounded approachable, perhaps the fact that she was offering some help may have been a trigger.

His discharge from the Army must have been stressful. Let's see how it starts tomorrow.

Jean called Lizzie. Typically, the phone was busy, so she left a message. 'Seeing Glen tomorrow will let you know how it goes.'

Meeting Glen. The Start

Jean made sure that she was at the pub well before the agreed time just to make sure she was not in a rush at the first meeting. Keep cool and in control, she thought, Glen may still be in Army mode.

Jean was hoping to have heard from Lizzie before the meeting with Glen. She pulled off Maldon Road into the pub car park. She was early, of course, but that was OK. She read over the notes she had made in regard to how she wanted to manage the interview. Initially, she would just ask a few questions and see how much Glen would talk.

She had used the sort of 'reflection' approach in previous meetings. Just retell or repeat what the client had said to help them feel that you were on their wavelength. She knew how to do it.

She ordered a wine and was sitting patiently when she noticed a man walk in. He was obviously Glen. Short hair, upright stance and shoulders back, still in the Army! He had recognised her red coat and gave a nod. Jean responded with a smile and a small wave. Wow, she thought, he is certainly an attractive man. Good looks and a good stance, surely he couldn't have killed Mia?

Glen approached her. 'Hello, you must be Jean the Redcoat! I'm Glen. Pardon the pun, but the Redcoats is what the soldiers of old England were called back in the 1600's. We did a bit of army history in our training.'

Now that is interesting, thought Jean, a memory for history. I wonder if the problems that he had in the Army were related to his upbringing. I'll find out.

'Can I get you a beer?'

'Thank you, Jean, a pint of bitter.' Jean got the beer and sat back down.

'Did you enjoy the history part of your training?'

'Certainly did. I found it quite fascinating to see how people were treated back then. In the 1600's army life as a Redcoat was pretty harsh. Certainly not like now, but there again, things have changed for the better too.'

'I can see that you certainly carry yourself very well. It is clear that Army life has left its mark. Do you think it was for you?' Jean was hoping that Glen would talk about the issues that led to his medical discharge or at least give an opening for her to slowly discover what happened.

'To be honest, at the start, I think it was. I was only about 19, and home life had not been the best, so I hoped that I could make new friends and discover a new life. That was my aim, anyway. At the start, it seemed to go well. I was amongst a lot of recruits who were going through the same experiences. The usual things away from home, which I didn't miss anyway, new rules, new contacts or friends, and new regulations. All of that stuff was going through your mind all the time.

Some of the guys were totally lost and didn't know what to do. You felt sorry for the quiet guys, they were picked on, mainly by the bullies. It used to annoy me so I was often breaking up a fight or making them stop bullying. As you can imagine, that got me into a bit of trouble, especially with the officers who seemed to think that I had started it.'

Glen seemed to have found his confidence. He certainly wasn't holding back as he talked about his experiences.

'How much did the bullying annoy you?'

'Quite a bit, really. I just felt that we were all in this together, so we should at least help each other.'

'How long were you at Catterick? You did go to Catterick, didn't you?'

'Sure did. We did 3 months of initial training. Then, we were able to have a home visit, but I chose to stay at the base. There was nothing for me at home. A few of us stayed on base, and it was all pretty casual. We still went to mess for meals but could go off base as we wanted to. We went into town, went to the cinema, and had a few beers at the pub.'

'What happened after the initial training?'

'We go to what they call Phase 2. Trade training, and then we get posted to our regiment and continue our training before being deployed somewhere. I went into transport. Regulations prevent me from telling you where I was deployed, though. Secret posting.'

'Thanks for that info. It sounds very interesting and must have been for you too. Are you sorry that the discharge happened?'

'In a way, I would say yes. I remember the Psych explaining to me that many of the strange things that were happening to me were not caused by PTSD but more than likely back to my early childhood.'

'Yes, I have heard about the impact of what the Psych call RCT or Repressed Childhood Trauma.'

'Are you a Psych then?'

'No, no, not me. I did study sociology and psychology at uni but it just helps in my role with you to understand how things happen to people and how it may have impacted you. It can result in things like poor sleep or even strange pains, so these unexplained pains can represent childhood trauma. It is possible that in the Army, it may have been taken as a way of faking pains to get discharged.'

'Jean, do you realise that what you are mentioning is just what was happening to me! I didn't want to leave the Army, I was happy in my role, but then sometimes I would have a total memory loss. My Officers thought that I was acting stupid to try to get a discharge. It was awful. I would have complete memory loss or memory gaps. It was a bit frightening, too. Especially when you get concentration problems and worst of all self-sabotaging thoughts. I wanted to break a leg so that I could go to hospital. It was crazy. So do you think that you can help me?

'I think I can, but I will need to look at your discharge papers. Are you able to let me see them?'

'They are at my house. I'll call you when I get back and make time to catch up again. Thank you so much for your help. I feel better already.'

'Thank you for your time, Glen. It has been so good to end up at this point. I'm excited, too, about how I can help. Look forward to your call, and my mobile number is on the card. Look forward to catching up again.'

Glen stood up and shook hands with Jean. A gentle handshake, conscious of not squeezing too firmly. After Glen had left Jean sat down and messaged Lizzie, 'Hi, had a good meeting with Glen. He is very open to talking. So much more to come. Meeting soon to view his discharge papers. Jean.'

Jean looked forward to the next message from Glen regarding the discharge papers. She had actually never seen discharge papers before so this may add to her learning.

Angela Calls

Jean felt her mobile vibrate in her handbag. It was Angela again. 'Hi, I've got some free time now, and I'm free until tomorrow afternoon, so I would love to catch up soon?'

'Good idea. I'm just in our old favourite pub, The White Hart in Witham. I was on my way home and just fancied stopping in for a wine. I'll meet you here if that suits you.?'

'Great, our old watering hole, if I remember correctly. I'm in the car now. See you soon.'

Jean felt a little tingle of excitement run through her. Why would Angela want to meet here again? Old memories I suppose.

Same for me, why was I such a silly lady to leave her in the first place? Our intimate life was beyond just good. Maybe we can come together again .… Jean sat back in her chair, having her wine, thinking about what could be. She was free tonight as well, so who knows? Then there is Carol to consider. I shall need to get things moving along quickly. Where would I like this to go?

Anyway, the first thing that I need to do is get the Glen thing in my head and see where it goes.

Jean pulled out her notebook. What I need to do is ask myself some simple questions to make sense of the last chat with Glen.

1. Why was he so quick to join the Army? Maybe if his home life was not too good, he was happy to join up as soon as possible

2. Lizzie's notes did not mention a family discussion. Maybe if his father ruled the roost then he laid down the rules and told Glen to join up or else.

3. He made that brief comment about his family life: 'There was nothing for me at home.' I wonder if Carol

can throw any light on what happened around that time. After all, she was 14.

4. Then, the discussion around the Repressed Childhood Trauma and his acknowledgement that I was really helping him. That is a serious issue.

5. All are coming to something. What were Glen's movements around Fyfield prior to going to the Army?

6. Who signed off on the medical certificate in relation to his medical state? Was it purely medical with no mental assessment?

7. Jean knew that she had to work through these questions. But next needed to see what was up with Angela.

Awaiting Angela

She put the notebook away and relaxed back in her nicely padded chair. She began to feel a little excited as she waited. It had been a while since she had enjoyed the closeness of Angela as a lover. Yet she wondered why Angela was so intent on seeing her now with what seemed a rather urgent request.

She was aware that Angela would sometimes become extremely anxious. She could withdraw so quickly with no explanation, just shut down. She was seemingly irrational, worried about what people would say and how they might judge her. Well,

I'll just see.

'Hi, how are you?'

Jean jumped in her chair and turned around. Angela was standing there. 'Crikey, you gave me a start, I was miles away.'

'I could see that, in fact, I even thought that you were nodding off…too much wine?'

Jean stood up. 'Not really, just deep in thought. Give me a hug.'

They both reached out and hugged, maybe for a little longer than just a plain hello type of hug!! This was an I want you to hug. It was plain to both of them that they had some unresolved feelings for each other. They both felt the shared emotional tension.

'Jean, we need to talk before we get carried away. Let me just get a wine, and I'll tell you what I feel concerned about.'

Angela returned with her wine and sat near to Jean. 'Let me fill you in on what has happened. I first met Carol at one of my Group Surveys on Family Breakdowns. To cut a long story short, she took a turn, and I ended up driving her home. She was too groggy to drive. She told me her husband had died, and I took it that I could stay. We ended up in bed together. Sorry, but we did.

Honestly, I asked her which bed I should sleep in, and she simply hugged me and said, 'Mine and that was that.'

I know next to nothing about her or what happened to her husband. Obviously, we didn't talk about that when we were in bed. We had an amazing night together, and the next morning, she said she wanted more of me. Well, with Uni commitments and so on, it was a few days before we could get together again.

Well, the next time we met, she was so excited. Not just because of seeing me, but she told me about meeting a lady called Evelyn who was having an affair with a man called George. It turned out to be Carol's husband. Now, they met in the graveyard at St. Mary's Church in High Ongar. Evelyn was about to pour a teapot of urine over his grave and smash the teapot.

'Does any of this make sense to you?' Jean nodded. 'Good. It turns out that Carol goes there once a week to shout curses at George's grave. So, between them, they had some sort of cleansing ritual and then went to the Foresters Arms for a drink and chat.

So I asked her, 'How did Evelyn know where George was buried, who told her, and where does Evelyn live?' She couldn't tell me anything!!'

'Good Lord Angela, what else did Carol tell her? I mean, was there anything about you? Did she not think about your reputation at Uni?' 'That's just what I said, and she nearly burst into tears.'

Jean's phone rang. She looked at the caller ID and said, 'Sorry, I have to answer this. Hello Glen, this is Jean. Did you manage to find the discharge papers?'

'Certainly did. I can go through them with you. Are you OK to meet at The White Hart again about 3 pm on Thursday?'

'I'll just check the diary. Yep, all ok. See you then. Thanks and Take care. Jean hung up and turned to Angela, 'Sorry about that, but I needed an answer. A new client. Tell me more.'

'That's OK. So, do you know anything about who this Evelyn may be? She is obviously not a friend of Carol's.'

'No, she certainly isn't a friend of Carol's. The meeting at the graveyard must have been their first meeting and a coincidence. I am somewhat bewildered by this turn of events. Carol was married to George, but the relationship was rather strained. From what I can deduce from my initial meetings is that he was a narcissist. She had a terrible marriage, and her whole life was miserable.

The strange thing is that Evelyn had obviously also met George and must have started a relationship with him. But how in the hell did she meet him?

Jean had a quizzical look on her face. 'I know Evelyn, and she is a client and supporter of my orphanage. But what concerns me more than anything is just how Evelyn managed to find out where George was buried despite the fact that I had previously tried to trace him…. with no luck.

Then, out of the blue, she sends me a bloody message just saying, 'Police advise George is dead. Have found the grave etc etc. Who would have done that?'

'Only somebody who knows her?'

Chapter 16
Evelyn's Story

Is it the Truth?

Evelyn pulled up into her drive, parked the car, and wandered into the house. She smiled to herself realising that she had really enjoyed the chat and the drinks with Carol. Another visit to The Foresters Arms is warranted, she thought, especially with Carol. What an interesting lady.

Thinking about the outcome of the day, she wondered how two people could have such totally different lives. First of all, Carol is living a rather miserable life with George, the narcissistic husband, and yet there is Evelyn living a beautiful life with Michael until he dies, of course.

What happens to people? Would her relationship with George have slowly slipped into the narcissistic relationship that Carole had endured? Maybe the fact that Carol pushed him down the stairs had saved her life in a way.

The more she thought about it, the more Evelyn realised she was facing a serious personal dilemma.

It wasn't that Carol had simply told her that she pushed George down the stairs and was responsible for his death. No, it was more in the way that she said it in such a dismissive way.

Almost in a 'well I just killed him' sort of way!! So knowing this may be true Evelyn wondered what does she do? But did Carol really push him, or did she just wish that she had pushed him? After all, she had lived a life of what could only be called pain, plus no doubt coping with a series of repressed emotions.

Should she now tell Graham? She realised that this was going to torment her for a while. After all, Graham had been kind to her over the George incident, especially telling her where George was buried. Damn, she thought, what would Michael tell her to do.

She hardly slept that night, and in the morning, waking with rather bleary eyes, Evelyn rose with thoughts swirling around in her head. What should she do? Should she get involved anyway? Maybe just a quick chat with Graham and see what he thinks.

She stared at the kettle as she made her morning cup of green tea..... The steam aimlessly left the spout and drifted upwards. The reality is that the problem she faces is quite clear in her mind. She is in possession of information that may lead to the conviction of a killer. But was Carol in her right mind? Had she endured years of torment? Did she really do it? She was using her old reporter's skills again.

Evelyn sipped on her tea as she stared across her garden.

The tulips, those beautiful tulips….. of course…... that's it …..She realised that if she did nothing, she would never be able to let it go and move on. She would always wonder….. just like she would have wondered about what happened to George….. if Graham hadn't told her, she would still be wondering to this day…… She picked up her phone and called Graham.

He answered in his police voice, 'Hello, Graham Williams, how can I help?'

'Graham, it's Evelyn, I need to talk to you about Carol Mitchell. Can you talk now?'

'Anything serious?'

'Well, I need to tell you this, or else I will forever wonder if I was withholding information……I happened to meet Carol Mitchell a couple of days ago at George's grave. We had a chat and then decided that the best thing to do was to bring on a Cleansing Session where she leveled curses at him, and I smashed a teapot full of urine over the grave. Then we decided to head to The Foresters Arms for a drink and chat.'

'Sounds like a fun moment.'

'Yes, it was, but as we were leaving, she turned to me and said that she was glad she had killed him. I just said pardon, and she said, 'I didn't mean to'……. I pushed him, and he fell down the stairs. Nothing further was said and we went to The Foresters.

Do I need to come in and make a statement?'

'Evelyn, I'll get back to you on that. Thank you anyway. Talk soon, take care.'

Graham hung up, leaving Evelyn feeling much better and relieved that she had at least done the right thing.

She picked up her cup of tea and wandered into the garden. The old oak tree held out its welcoming branches as Evelyn sat down. Alone again ……. reflecting on the last few months.

The time with George, the closeness they had developed, his tenderness and passion. She smiled as she thought about how they would laugh together, the cups of tea in bed on a weekend morning. She realised that their sex was so much a part of their happy relationship. He was a beautiful lover. Now she just felt used. Yes, George had made her feel wonderful. She had never had orgasms like she did when she was with him.

She thought of Michael and almost felt as if she had let him down and been unfaithful. Life with him was so gentle and happy. They may not have been mad, crazy lovers, but their loving was intense, passionate and beautiful.

She felt angry with Carol for what she did, robbing her of a possible happy future when she killed George.

Holy hell … Stop it Evelyn …..what a stupid thought…..He was a damned narcissist……. It would never have been a happy future, much like what happened to Carol. George was just waiting to perhaps move in with her, and then things would change. Yes …. That was it really…. Sort of the calm before the storm.

Now, she felt angry at being made to feel so foolish. No more, No more relationships. No more being manipulated. George seemed to be so charming, but he was always lying. His whole life with Carol and me was a lie.

The voice in her head kept saying, 'Let it go, Evelyn, let it go. He was cheating on both you and Carol. He was controlling, he was lying.'

Evelyn let out a shout followed by a long sigh, and finally …….. she just felt relaxed. …. That's better, she thought. Life must go on. I'll pop into Epping later and go to the markets. Nothing like a bit of shopping to get the mind in shape.

As she sat and thought about the past weeks, Evelyn realised she hadn't seen Jean for a while either. They should catch up so that she can explain how she found out about what happened to George and how she met Carol. I'll call her when I get back.

The car accident.

Evelyn put on her shopping dress and comfortable walking shoes. Picking up her handbag and shopping bag, she headed to the car. As she got in, she was deep in thought about Jean and hoping that she would be OK when she found out about how Graham had helped her sort out the George issue.

Driving down Willingale Road, she neared the intersection with the A414 taking her to Epping.

The police report says that she must have driven through the stop sign before realising that the truck on her side of the road was too near and unable to stop.

The collision resulted in her instant death, the driver of the truck was in shock but not injured….

Graham Williams was in Epping police station when he heard the police radio report. 'Fatal car accident at the intersection of A414 and Willingale Rd near Norton Heath.' He jumped out of his chair and ran to the radio room.

'What was the registration of the car in the A414 accident?'

'Not sure yet, sir, but it was a single occupant, older lady. Police on site advise that she is known to them and lives in Norton Heath. Ambulance and equipment on their way.'

Graham pulled up a chair and sat down. His instincts told him that it had to be Evelyn. He felt utterly shocked and saddened. He was going to call her this afternoon. He needed to talk to her about the comment that Carol had made to her when they were in the graveyard.

Maybe she had her mind filled with what had been going on in her life over the last couple of weeks. Just not concentrating. She was probably thinking about George dying or going to the grave and meeting Carol or finding out that Carol may have killed George.

He decided to call Evelyn's mobile, just in case he was wrong. But he wasn't wrong. Evelyn was dead. Tears came into his eyes as he walked slowly back to his desk with a feeling of emptiness and sadness inside him. He just felt numb. The loss of such a lovely lady was terrible but now, in her memory, he was determined to find out just what went on with Carol and George.

Chapter 17

The Chatter

Changing Times

Jean picked up her local paper to read over breakfast. Horror hit her. The news of Evelyn's death was on the front page of the local paper.

Mrs Evelyn Parker, late of Norton Heath, was killed yesterday in a car accident on the A414 near Norton Heath. She will be remembered as the lady who loved her tulips.

Married to Michael Parker [dec'd], solicitor, they both worked tirelessly to help local children build their lives and their futures to avoid a custodial sentence or a fine. A service will be held at St Mary's Church, High Ongar. Friends and Family Welcome. See web site for details.

Jean read it and re-read it as she began to cry. 'Evelyn, my dear Evelyn, my orphanage supporter.'

Jean's phone rang. It was Carol. 'Have you heard the news? The lady that was killed in the car accident was Evelyn. She is the lady that I met at George's grave. She was lovely. The poor lady ended up with George, but only for a while.

We talked to each other at the grave, then went to The Foresters for a drink and chat. She was so sweet.

I'm shattered, Jean, I've been crying all morning. I just wish Angela would call, and I need to see her so much. Gosh, I want that woman.' 'You and me both.'

'What do you mean?

'Oh, nothing. She helps me with managing my stress. I have therapy sessions with her. I'll be in touch soon. We should talk more.

Before you go, I just want to ask if Evelyn happened to mention how she found out that George was dead and where he was buried?'

'No, she didn't tell me. Funny that you asked me that because Angela asked me too. The only thing that I can guess is that she must have known someone in the local police. Talk to me soon. I'm missing you.'

'We'll talk soon. Take care.'

Jean hung up quickly realising that Carol may start to ask too many questions. The next call was to Angela. She dialled Angela's number.

'Hello Jean, what a nice early morning call, wish you were here.'

'Well in a way, it would be nice if I was there, and I wish I was, but I have some, maybe, good but sad news for you. Evelyn was killed in a car accident yesterday. It appears that she may have been on her way to Epping, probably shopping.'

'Oh God, that is terrible, but I hate to say this, what luck and a cruel ending to our dilemma.'

'Let's hope so. Anyway must go. Another meeting later. Take care, I want you.'

Jean hung up. Holy hell, she thought, what is happening to me?

She checked her calendar. The meeting with Glen was scheduled for this afternoon. She decided that today was going to be both a reflective day and a sad day too.

Meeting Glen

Jean sat, with her wine, in her favourite spot in the White Hart hotel, waiting for Glen. She wondered just what she might unearth within the discharge papers that Glen was going to provide to her. Was his discharge based on his mental issues or something to do with a possible violent outbreak?

She had carried out a little research on medical discharges, but it had seemed that the final decisions and reasons would be in the 'discharge papers.'

Let's just wait and see she thought.

The door to the private bar opened and in walked Glen, still carrying himself like a well-trained soldier. Head up and shoulders back.

'Glen, Hi. Come take a seat. Can I get you a beer?'

'Yes, please. The usual. A pint of bitter.' Jean returned to the table with a beer and a wine.

'So tell me, what interesting comments are in your discharge papers?'

'Well, you have a read and see what you think. I certainly went through a thorough shakedown when the first reports started to go in about me.'

'What sort of process did you go through, or is it easier for me to read through the papers first?'

'Well, I made a copy so you can read in your own time and take in what you feel. You may understand a bit more about me that way and see what was involved.'

'That sounds like a good idea. So you start by telling me what you want.'

Glen and Mia

Glen took a sip of his beer, sat back in his chair, and took a deep breath. Jean wondered what was going to come out. She felt intrigued, especially as Lizzie had told her that she may not want Glen as a client. So what was it that made Lizzie feel he may be the killer?

Glen leaned forward, 'Well, first, I hated living at home on the farm. My father was a real bully. He would use his leather belt on me and knock my Mum around. I was too small to stop him and couldn't do anything about it when he got into his rages.

I would run and hide in the cattle feed sheds but he would find me, and I would get a beating. I think I was about 5 when he started to beat Mum. Carol had just been born.'

Jean listened with a sense of horror running through her. My God, the small child would have been terrified. Glen continued with what seemed to be his life story. Tears began to form in his eyes as he talked about Carol.

'I hated it when he would come home smelling of drink. He would go into Carol's room. She would have been about 12. I could hear her crying.'

Glen was crying. Was it a feeling of guilt that he couldn't stop his father, just as he couldn't stop him hitting his Mother?

'Glen is that why you wanted to join the army? To get away from the house and the horrors that you were feeling?'

Glen leaned forward and put his head in his hands. 'No. I had wanted to leave a long time before. It meant that I could get away from the house after I turned 19. After I left school, I worked on the farm but after I caught my father, he told me to go and join up and not to come back.'

'Caught your father what?'

'Down by the river.'

'Doing what?'

'He was with a girl, I think. It looked like he was having sex with her. He was a big, strong man and he was holding her down. He was on top of her. I was crossing the river when I saw him. He shouted and I ran away to the sheds to hide. But he found me. He could always find me. He came at me with his belt, but this time he didn't hit me. He just spoke and said to get out and join the army and never come back again.

I had talked about joining the army after I turned 19 so I went to the Chelmsford Army Recruitment Centre and ended up in the Catterick Army Base.'

Jean stood up, 'Let me get you another beer because I certainly need another wine.'

Jean felt the need to get her breath. What she had just heard from Glen would shatter Lizzie. It seemed obvious that Glen had seen his father raping Mia.

She needed to talk further to Glen to see if he remembered anything else that would help in solving the death of Mia. She also realised that the next step would be to read the Discharge Documents.

There may be some information in there regarding his Repressed Childhood Trauma, after all, Glen had spoken openly about the beatings that he received from his father. And how the hell had he coped with his father molesting Carol when she was only 12.

This trauma must have devastated him, plus the guilt he felt in leaving both of them alone with his father.

Jean walked back towards the table, thinking that she needed to ring Lizzie this evening or preferably as soon as she arrived home.

'Glen, can we meet again after I have had time to read through the Discharge Papers? I would like to really understand how the Army psych understood you. That way, I can help you in a more effective way.'

'That's fine Jean. Any help is much appreciated. There is no love lost between my father and me. However, I do worry about my mum. I haven't seen Carol for a long time and would like to catch up with her eventually.'

'Thank you. I'll read through the DP's and get back to you. Take Care.'

Chapter 18
Lizzie Hurley

Finding Mia's Killer

Jean drove home slowly, her mind swirling with thoughts of how confused and disturbed Glen must be. She thought to herself that the only way he could handle his tormented and damaged childhood and, eventually his youth was to repress those memories.

But just what impact would that repression have had on him as he grew up? He seemed so well-balanced when talking about his past. He spoke about the beatings as if they were just not hurtful. Rather matter of fact. It just happened, so what?

Jean wondered then if perhaps not everyone exposed to childhood trauma developed a mental illness, although it may increase the risk. Maybe he was just resilient and no doubt his time in the army may have helped him.

Anyway, let's see what the DPs say. I need to call Lizzie. Jean sat in her armchair and called Lizzie who strangely answered promptly.

'Hi, what news?'

'Well, what do you want? The story so far or a precis?'

'Give me just the abbreviated version.'

'OK, but you may want to sit down as I tell you. …. Oh crikey. I'll go straight to the real issue. …. Glen had decided to join the army. After leaving school, he worked on the farm until he turned 19. He hated being at home and was keen to get away. The army was his solution. He was walking home one day to cross over The River Roding to the family farm near Fyfield.'

'As he crossed over, he saw his father with a girl. He was lying on top of her, and he thought he was having sex with her. He couldn't see the girl. His father yelled out, and Glen ran to the farm's cattle feed sheds, where he used to hide. His father found him but didn't belt him this time, just telling him to join the army and never come back.'

'Christ, are you telling me that it was Glen's father who may have killed Mia?'

'Possibly, more than likely, and I suspect yes….. but I can't believe that the police didn't ever investigate the family. The old man just lied. Glen was already in the army by the time Mia's body was discovered, so the old man probably told them Glen wasn't around and got away with it.'

'Lizzie, I have a copy of Glen's Army Discharge Papers. I haven't read them yet, as he only gave them to me this afternoon. Don't do anything until I have had a chance to read through them.

As soon as I have read through and made my notes I'll call you. Probably tomorrow morning. My feeling is that we may be near to finding out who did it. The problem is that this is now a cold case, and we need some forensic evidence to reopen the case.'

'OK, and thank you. By the way, do you have any contacts with the police because we may need to talk to the original detectives if they are still alive?'

'Till tomorrow.'

Jean knew that she would have to face Carol sooner or later, so she might as well call now to make a time. However, she needed to leave a bit of time to read over Glen's Discharge Papers. I'll send a text message.

'Hi, Carol. Hoping to catch up with you soonish. Have some interesting things to run over with you. Let me know when you are free. Jean'

Jean put the phone down and picked up the envelope containing the copies of Glen's Discharge Papers. This may make for some interesting reading, she thought.

The Discharge Papers.

Jean opened up the envelope. She had never seen discharge papers before so she took the time to read carefully through each page.

She saw that Glen had actually enlisted in the Army, meaning that he would serve without delay following his training. The UK Army discharge papers include all the information to help soldiers leave the army 'in an orderly manner.'

There were the expected documents, ID Certificates, references for employment, local contact details, Pay and kit allowances to show that all allowances had been settled, full names, rank, and so on.

Jean was looking for a medical report or a psych assessment, but there didn't seem to be one.

However, she noticed that Glen had been given a medical discharge instead of a general one. But where were the medical records or even the psych test results?

From her research, she deduced that Medical discharges are exclusively given to people who **became ill or injured during their military service** and cannot perform the duties required of productive Armed Forces members.

This type of administrative discharge is unique because it requires service members to undergo a medical evaluation and careful assessment of their cases. It needs to be proven that the military member has become unable to fulfill their obligations because of their military service period. In select cases, military service causes a pre-existing condition to get worse.

This, without a doubt, would apply to Glen. His childhood trauma would potentially contribute to various mental illnesses in adults, including post-traumatic stress disorder (PTSD), anxiety disorders, depression, and borderline personality disorder (BPD). The severity and type of mental illness may vary depending on the nature, duration, and frequency of the trauma, as well as the individual's genetic predisposition and coping mechanisms.

From her time studying psych she knew that the brain's attempt to protect itself from painful memories can also lead to gaps in memory regarding childhood events.

Is this what happened to Glen? Maybe he was in the middle of something, and he suffered a memory loss. This could prove dangerous if he is supposed to follow orders. It would not be unusual for senior officers to put in a report on his behaviour. Should there be a few reports then the Medical Officer was likely to examine him, leading possibly to a psych assessment, which ultimately may lead to a discharge.

Without the results being available Jean would have to surmise that is how the discharge was affected.

But for her, there was a lingering doubt that he may have manipulated the symptoms to suit his needs. In the back of her mind, she recalled how, during their initial meeting, he had been rather dismissive of any of the trauma that may have impacted him.

Interesting, she thought, but it was quickly followed by the thought of what he had been doing since his discharge. Looking at him, he may well have been suitable to time as a mercenary. She felt that maybe a further talk with Carol was needed.

Facing Carol Again

Jean knew that she had to face Carol again. Not only to find out what she may know about Glen and his leaving the army but also to see what had been going on with Angela.

After her last meeting with Angela, she felt that there may be a possibility of getting together again and a real chance to reconnect. She knew that she needed something more in her life, and Angela would fill that something.

She called Carol, who had by now acquired a mobile and had shared the number with all of her contacts.

'Hi Carol, it's Jean.'

'Oh, I'm so pleased that you called. I want to catch up with you again. When can we meet?'

'Well, I'm over near Chelmsford. I can meet you soon if I leave now.'

'That's good. See you soon. I'll put the kettle on.'

Jean hung up and stayed sitting on her chair. How will I handle this? Two things that I need to understand more clearly.

One is what does she know about Glen leaving the army and two, she needs to find out how the hell did Evelyn find out about George's gravesite. This was really concerning to her. Mind you, she would let Carol bring up Angela if it was in her mind. There was no point in stirring the hornet's nest if there were no hornets.

She picked up her bag and went to the car, opening the driver's side door to get in. From her back seat came a voice.

'Hello, Jean.' She recognised it immediately. It was Glen. She froze.

'Glen, what are you doing?'

'Maybe I should be asking you that question?'

'What do you mean?'

'The meetings, the questions, my papers. You don't really want to help, do you? That is not what this is all about, is it? Who put you on to me? Was it Carol or Lisbeth Hurley?'

Jean felt her heart pounding. Her mouth had gone dry, and her hands were sweating. She didn't know what to do or what to say. Something like this had never happened to her before. She was always the one in control, the one who had all the answers. She was trying to speak, but the words wouldn't come out.

'Glen, I ….'

'Shut up and listen to me. I didn't kill Mia. It was probably my father. Mia was a friend of Carol's, she was only 12, like Carol. They used to meet down by the river because Mia was too afraid to come to the house. She was afraid of my father. They were two beautiful little girls. The only real friend that Carol had when they were in junior school together.'

'Glen, I honestly didn't know that about Mia. Why do you think that your father killed her anyway?'

'Because she was the girl he was raping when I saw him. Do you have any idea of what he was doing to Carol? I couldn't do anything to stop it, Jean. He was too strong for me. I feel sick every time I think about it. I wanted to kill him, but I couldn't. Carol was 14 when he raped her one night. After that, she changed a lot.'

Jean felt the tears forming behind her eyes. She could hear the sadness mixed with anger in Glen's voice. What was he going to tell her? What was he going to do to her?

'Glen, let me explain something to you. I only met Carol after she went to the Coroners Court over George's death. A friend of mine who worked in the Court had seen her and asked me to help her. I didn't know about you until she told me that she had a brother. She didn't remember much about you because you had been sent to join the army.'

'What else did she tell you about me?'

'Nothing. She didn't say anything other than she remembers you going away to join the army. Like you, she remembers that she wanted to get away from that house. She left school and went into nursing. She lived at the hospital in Epping. I'm supposed to be meeting her now. She is waiting for me. Do you know what has happened to her since you left?'

'Of course I do. Who do you think pushed George down the stairs? Carol is quite right when she says that she was in the kitchen. She was.

But she was also so traumatised when he was alive that she couldn't remember anything clearly or properly. She wishes that she had pushed him because she wanted him dead, so much so that she now believes that she did push him, which is why she seems so happy. Give me your phone. …. Please.'

He scrolled through previous calls and rang Carol. Before Carol could say anything, Glen spoke. 'It's my fault that Jean is running late. We needed to talk, but she was on her way now. Take care. Love you and talk soon.'

He handed back her phone and stepped out of the car. 'So, you can tell Mia's sister that it was my father who killed Mia, but how you will come up with new evidence, I don't know. Try talking to Sgt. Graham Williams at Epping Police Station. Sorry if

I scared you.'

He turned and walked away before Jean could speak. She took a deep breath and let her body rhythm settle back down. God, that was a scare, she sighed.

Chapter 19

Lisbeth Hurley

Notes from Jean

Before she drove to Carol's house she just had to call Lizzie.

'Lizzie, it's Jean. Listen to me, and I just need to tell you this. I'm driving, and I've just had a serious talk with Glen. Mind you, he broke into my car and scared the living daylights out of me. And thank you, I am OK now!!'

'From what he told me, he must have been living in the area incognito. I'll fill you in on a couple of other things when we next meet, but the outcome of our last discussion is that he believes his father killed Mia. He must have raped her down by the river when Glen saw him with a girl. That was the catalyst for him joining the army.'

'I've read through some of his discharge papers, and there is nothing there about any mental issues. It's possible that there may be a separate report on those issues. Mind you, after my meetings with him, I would assess him as sane but still a very controlled person.'

'I have yet to find out what he was doing between leaving the army and returning here. Anyway, I am heading over to Carol's place to dig around a bit more about her father, although I suspect she has not seen him since she left to go nursing. I'll need to move quickly so we can get to him before he dies, which could be soon if

Glen is in the area. Nearly at Carol's. Call you later.'

Talk about Glen

Jean arrived at Carol's house but with a slightly more enquiring mind. She now wondered about Carol's mental state. The poor lady had suffered a pretty sad and traumatic life. And here was Glen saying that he had pushed George down the stairs. To do that, he must have been hiding in the house, maybe hiding in one bedroom. I'll find out from Carol, but that assumes that Glen was telling the truth.

There just seems to be so much twisted so-called 'truth-telling.' Thank heavens that Evelyn didn't find out too much about Carol. Poor Evelyn. What a sad outcome for such a beautiful lady.

Jean knocked on the front door. Carol's smiling face was there to greet her. 'Hello, come on in. Tea is ready. Did Glen hold you up for long?'

'Not really, but that is OK. He told me a few things that I needed to know. By the way, are you in for the night or going out later?'

'I'm in for the night. Why do you ask?'

'Well, I would like to spend some time talking about your brother Glen and yourself if you feel comfortable. I'm not sure how much you know about his life. You were quite young when he left and joined the army. Do you remember those days?'

'Oh yes. The thing that I remember most was when Daddy got angry with Glen and told him to go away. Mia and I were playing at my house, and she left to go home. Mia was afraid of my daddy. She left to go home and never came back to play with me. I don't know why she didn't come back to see me. Daddy went to look for her but said he couldn't find her. That was the day that I heard Daddy shouting at Glen to leave the house, join the army, yes and there we go and never come back again. He left a few days later, and I never saw him again.'

'Did he ever come and stay with you and George here in Epping Green?'

'Why do you ask that?'

'I just wondered. Maybe he missed you or wanted to make sure that you were safe.

Would George have let him into the house?'

'Oh no. George didn't like Glen, so he wouldn't like him at the house.'

'So when did George first meet Glen?'

'I'm not sure, but I think he did.'

'Carol, you do know that you can tell me the truth, don't you?'

'Jean, I'm afraid of things. Sometimes, when George was away, Glen would come and stay with me. I was afraid of being on my own in the dark. I was afraid that Daddy would come into the house. When I was little, It was in the dark that Daddy would come into my bed and hurt me and make me cry. George used to hurt me, too.'

'Was Glen here when George fell down the stairs?'

'Yes, George came home late after one of his trips away for work. He didn't know that Glen was already in his bedroom. In the morning, I made breakfast and a cup of tea for George. I think Glen made him fall down the stairs.'

Jean sat back in the chair and sipped her tea, which was slowly going cold. She couldn't believe what Carol was telling her but it fitted in with what Glen had mentioned earlier. Oh no, Angela, she thought, you can't become involved with Carol, it will utterly ruin your reputation once this all ends up in Court somehow.

'Carol, where did Glen go after George fell down the stairs?'

'I don't know. As he came downstairs, he just said that he would call the ambulance, and then he told me not to tell anybody that he had been in the house. So I didn't. I just said that George fell. Is that a problem?'

'No, not really, as long as you remember that. Have the police been to see you again?'

'Yes. Sergeant Williams called in again to see if I was OK.'

'That's good. Did he happen to mention which station he was from?'

'His card said Epping Police Station.'

'I don't suppose you have the card by any chance?'

'Yep. Here it is. He said to call him if I had any problems, but I don't have any really. I just hope Angela contacts me soon. I miss her.'

Jean had a quick brain flash. Well, keep missing her Carol, because I'm not going to let you get near her.

'Just a thought, Carol. Did I ever mention my orphanage project? Angela is a big supporter. I ask my clients to go to the website and donate to help the kids in the orphanage. Would you like to help? I can send the link to you.'

'Yes, I would like to help. You have been such a big help to me. I would like to support others, especially now that I have

George's money.'

Just what I thought. Jean couldn't believe that she had just blurted that out to Carol. Not only that but it was so easy to gain another supporter. She hadn't ever looked at the orphanage bank account, but she felt that there was a fair amount in there by now. She was often tempted to look at the account but she remembered that the initial strategy was to not look at the balance until she felt that she needed the money. That would be the time she would withdraw the money and have to disappear or leave England altogether. Or maybe not?

Before she left, she realised that she still needed to talk to Carol a bit more about Glen.

'Carol, can I ask you a bit more about Glen?

'What do you want to ask Jean?'

Jean spun around at the sound of Glen's voice.

'Glen, I didn't realise that you were here. I want to talk to you. Will you let me ask a few questions? You can say no if you don't want to answer.'

'OK. Ask away.'

'Perhaps I should first fill you in on the background. The death of Mia has become what the police call a Cold Case. Essentially, a Cold Case is a crime that has not been solved and is not currently under investigation. However, if some new evidence is found, then it can be reopened with modern-day forensics, that is quite likely.

'The reason I wanted to talk with you is to see if you have any idea of any possible new evidence that could be located. For instance, if you think your father killed Mia, then would any clothing be hidden? Did he have a walking stick that he may have used to hit her? I know that may be difficult to think about, but you never know. You were right when you asked me in the car who had put me up to this. It was Lizbeth Hurley, Mia's sister. She didn't suspect you, and she just felt that you may know something that could help. And you do.'

'Has any of this been reported to the police yet?'

'No, that is also why I wanted to speak to you first. I want to make sure that if we go to the police with some more information then both you and Carol are not going to be dragged through with more questioning. So what I need to know is what happened to you after you left the Army? What did you do?'

'I can't tell you very much except that I was involved with an organisation known as Dark Justice. You can find the website and see what we did. We weren't the TV series!! We were formed in 2014 and disbanded in 2021. We operated mainly in the north of England, which is why Carol did not know anything about me. Our main objectives were to catch paedophiles, and we succeeded in catching over 150.'

'So that is what I was doing until I came down here and contacted Carol. I found out a lot about what Carol had gone through with George so I was determined to put a stop to it but not sure how. In the end, the 'push down the stairs' was so simple that it was child's play. For Carol, it was life-changing and so I went away again. Nobody will ever be able to prove otherwise that George didn't trip.'

'But back to Mia. I will do my best to try to uncover some new evidence. I may even take the step of confronting my father. He's getting on, and I suspect that when he sees me again, it may be 'heart attack time!!' As soon as I have so information I'll let you know.'

Call to Lizzie.

Jean left Glen and Carol at the house and drove home. The last couple of meetings had certainly been productive in setting some things on a clearer pathway. Jean felt that a meeting with Lizzie would be worthwhile so that they could have a sensible conversation. Following an uneventful drive home, Jean pulled into her driveway. Just past the end of her fence line, she noticed a car that wasn't familiar to her. She felt a bit uneasy especially following the recent surprises when she found Glen in the car!

She stepped out and walked into her garden, standing behind the tree near the gate. The car door opened, and Lizzie stepped out!

'Lizzie, what are you doing here? I was just going to call you.'

'I want to know what's going on. Have you had any further talks with Glen?'

'That's where I have been. I left their place about 25 minutes ago. Funny that I should say 'their place' because it almost seems like that. Come on in, and I can give you the situation. I was going to call and say we should meet, anyway, you being here is good.'

'Jean, the last time we spoke you told me about reading through Glen's Discharge papers and stuff. So do you think he did it?'

'I'll cut out all the talking and stuff and tell you no. He tells me it was his father. He saw what he thought was his father having sex with maybe a girl. So, he leaves the house and joins the Army. Several years later, he has a medical Discharge and seems to disappear. The reason he seemed to disappear is that he joined an organisation up north called Dark Justice which traced and prosecuted paedophiles. He left there in 2021. I told you that Carol supposedly killed George, her husband, but she didn't. Glen did. He sometimes stays with Carol. Why doesn't it matter at the moment?

After several conversations, Glen tells me that it was his father who killed Mia.'

Now, I have the name of the police Sergeant who attended George's death inquiry and has been following up with Carol. More than likely because he thinks Carol pushed George down the stairs. Which she didn't because Glen did. So, my next step is to contact Sgt Williams to see if we can get some details of Mia's death. Glen is going to see if he can find any forensic evidence back at the house. Not sure how, but that will enable the police to open what is a cold case. We are near to discovering the killer Lizzie. So, how are you feeling now?

'Not sure, but we are certainly a long way ahead compared to last time. You have done a great job. Thank you. When do you feel we need to go to the police?'

'I'm not sure, but I'm going to type up some notes and the points I can give to the police. I don't want to expose Glen, though, because he will be the key to the killer.'

Jean was feeling a bit uneasy. Lizzie just seemed a bit, well, odd about the discussion. Almost as if she didn't care anymore. And why did she come to my house? She could have called my mobile. Jean felt that it was almost as if Lizzie didn't want the case solved. Am I right, she thought?

'Lizzie, I feel that you are not your usual vibrant self, what is the matter?'

'I haven't been able to let go of Mia for all these years. And now, as we seem to be getting closer to her killer, I feel as if I am going to miss her. Silly, isn't it but that's just the feeling I have. It has been as if Mia is still a part of me.'

'Lizzie, Mia will always be a part of you. Your dedication is a testament to your caring, and we will solve this for you.'

'I'm going Jean. Thank you. Talk again soon.' Lizzie turned towards the front door and left, leaving Jean somewhat perplexed about Lizzie's emotional state.

Angela Calls Again

Jean's phone rang. 'Jean, it's me, Angela. Are you at home? I'm coming over.'

'OK, I'll put the wine on ice. We need to have a drink together, I think. I hope you want to stay the night. See you soon.' Jean went and sat at her computer. She had to put some pointers together to present to Sgt. Graham Williams about the whole Mia incident, despite what Glen may discover in the meantime.

She opened her notebook. Never one to keep notes when she was with a client, she had developed an acute memory by always writing her notes when she arrived home. This made it easier for Sgt Williams.

Angela was going to be a while, so she felt it would be worthwhile calling Sgt. Williams now to make a time to meet.

She pulled out the card that Carol had given her and rang the number. Graham answered.

'Hello, this is Sgt Williams.'

'Hello, Sgt. This is Jean. We have never met but I am a friend of Carol Mitchell and also knew Evelyn Parker. I need to talk to you about the death of Mia Hurley. Can we make a time to meet, preferably away from the police station? I'm not sure if you know about Mia Hurley, but she died on the Spicers farm in Fyfield. I believe it is still a cold case. Carol Mitchell was Carol Spicer and was a close friend of Mia Hurley.'

'Whoa, whoa, hold on, Jean. Let's just arrange a meeting first, and you can fill me in when we meet. To reopen a cold case is not easy unless we have some more positive forensic evidence. Can you get to the Foresters Arms in High Ongar at about 3 pm tomorrow?

'Yes, that is OK for me. See you then. I'll have on a red coat and be in the Saloon. Joan closed her computer.

Graham hung up and turned to Ken, his constable. 'Well, you are never going to believe this. We have a meeting at 3 tomorrow at The Foresters Arms in High Ongar. The topic is… hold your breath… Mia Hurley, the cold case. The lady we are meeting knows Carol Mitchell and also knew Evelyn Parker. What's going on out there? Suppose we are going to find out. I might let the Chief Inspector know about this, but after the meeting. No point in stirring things up if the meeting turns out to be bullshit. It will be good for our records if we can solve this little murder.'

Next, Joan rang Lizzie. 'Hi Lizzie, just to let you know that I have set up a meeting with Epping Police at 3 pm tomorrow. The Sgt that I am meeting was involved with George Mitchell's death, that's Glen's brother-in-law. I'm talking to him about the process of opening a cold case. I don't expect to have any information from Glen by then so I'll chase him up later and let you know the outcome. Stay Happy.'

Angela visits.

Jean closed her computer just as there was a knock on the front door. Ah ha, she sighed, Angela, I hope. She opened the door slowly to create a sensual impact, almost as if she were reading Samuel Coleridge's poem Xanadu.

Jean looked at Angela, 'In Xanadu did Kubla Khan a stately pleasure dome decree, Where Alph the sacred river ran, Through caverns measureless to man, Down to a sunless sea."Do come in, my Lovely Lady, I hope you are feeling as I am?

Angela looked into Jean's eyes. 'If only you knew, but I'm hoping to let you know soon.'

Jean reached for Angela, pulling her slowly as close as she could so she could kiss her gently on the lips. Their hands reached for each other holding an extremely passionate embrace.

'Angela, the wine is on the ice, but maybe we should leave it until a bit later. I think a lot later.'

Jean felt her whole body quivering with beautiful excitement. She had already wrapped one leg around Angela's leg, thrusting their bodies into each other.

'Jean, take me to bed. I want your naked body next to me. I want to feel your lips all over me. I'm so ready to have you as you have me. A 69 would make me come so quickly.'

'Come on.' Jean took Angela by the hand and led her to the bedroom.

Their passion was finally spent, and they lay exhausted on the bed. As they lay beside each other, Angela rolled over to look at Jean. 'My God, you are such a deeply sensual lover, Jean, we can't stop this, it is so good for us.'

'I know, I don't want it to stop either. I'll get us a glass of wine. Just relax, my dear,' said Jean as she rose to fetch the wine.

'Alright,' sighed Angela.

Chapter 20
Glen's Story

A Sorry Tale

Glen sat in his car, looking at his watch. He knew the next few hours would probably be the hardest he had ever had to endure. Calling his Father. But it had to happen. He would take it slowly as he had no idea how his parents would react. They were both getting on in age, but the next steps had to be taken.

Glen rang and waited for the phone to be answered. A few rings and his Mother answered.

'Hello, this is Mrs. Spicer.'

'Hello, this is Glen Spicer.'

'Glen, oh Glen, where are you? Can you come to the house?'

'Yes, I'm not far away. If you are both at home, I can call in to say Hello.'

'Oh, that is wonderful. I'll wake your Father up; he is just having his nap. How long will you be?'

'About 20 minutes. See you soon.'

Glen hung up. *Oh well, that didn't go too badly*, he thought. *Lucky Mum answered the phone, I suppose.*

Whilst his Father was a bit distant and just shook his hand his dear Mum gave him a long and loving Hug. Glen looked at his Mum. Just like mothers do, He thought. They never stop loving their children.

Questions and stories flowed as Glen filled in his history. Mum and his Father sat listening, almost spellbound. Glen did omit a few little details, such as the George death issue, how Carol had been treated and a few other things that would have made his mum unhappy.

Eventually, Glen realised that the time had come when he had to bring up Mia's death.

Taking a deep breath, Glen said, 'I hear that the Epping Police are going to open the case of Mia Hurley's death. Do you remember her? She was Carol's friend who was found beside the river, having been raped and killed.'

'It appears that some new evidence has surfaced. With modern-day technology, the police believe that they can trace the DNA that they collected at the time so it can be matched with the new evidence. Did you ever have to provide DNA samples?'

Glen's parents looked at each other. 'Yes, we did, but never heard anything back.'

Glen wanted to make it clear to his Father how the new DNA would have been found.

'I'm not sure where it has come from but most likely it is from Mia's clothes. Her sister Lizzie kept all of the clothes she was wearing at the time she died. So, any contact with her killer would have left traces of DNA. The results are usually pretty conclusive these days. That was often how we caught the paedophiles when I was working with Dark Justice.'

Glen glanced at his watch, waiting for the pre-arranged phone call to ring on his mobile. He knew that he could trust Carol. Glen's mobile rang, and he answered. 'Hello, yes speaking. That's fine, Yes, Yes, That's OK I'll leave soon. Thanks.'

He turned to Mum. 'Sorry but I have to go. I'll be in touch again soon. Take care.' Glen stood up and turned to leave the house realising that this may be the last time that he saw his father alive. He wasn't sure if he really cared that much. Life with his father had been pretty awful.'

Old man Spicer watched his son walk towards the door. Under his breath, he whispered to himself, 'Sorry son, I'm so sorry, please forgive me.'

He turned, walked into the living room and sat at the writing desk. He knew that the time had come, he could no longer live with the guilt of his sins. He pulled out a sheet of paper and began to write.

These are my last words.

To Glen and Carol. As I have grown old, I have realised how much I must have hurt you. I am sorry. I have missed both of you all these years. Carol and Mia, I don't know why I hurt you. Please forgive me. I am sorry. My life has been a torment. God help me and save me from my sins. Cast me to Hell so I may rot in eternal damnation.

To my dear wife, I am sorry for how I treated you. I am a no-good, careless man. I didn't deserve you, and I hate myself for the things that I did to you.

To the police, I confess to raping and accidentally killing Mia Hurley. I do not know why I did that. I ask Mia's family to take pity on me and forgive me.

Archer Spicer.

With a simple fold of the paper, he placed the letter into an envelope and walked to the feeding shed. Taking the *410 in his hands he pointed the two barrels to his heart and pulled the trigger.

Mrs Spicer heard the blast and burst into tears knowing that what he had done finally saw that he had atoned for his sins.

Mrs Spicer ran to her phone and called Glen.

Glen let the phone ring twice and answered, knowing he didn't want to hear the news.

'Glen speak.......'

'Glen it's Mum. Your Father is dead. Come quickly. He did it himself. Quickly, come home soon. I need you here. I'll call the police.'

Glen hung up and went to his car, driving as quickly as he could to the farm.

Chapter 21
Sgt. Graham Williams

Spicer Suicide

Graham's phone rang. 'Hello, Graham Williams. Yes, The Fyfield Farm. OK, I know. Heading there now. Call the Ambulance.'

Graham turned to Ken, 'Well, here we go again. Looks like Old Man Spicer has committed suicide. I'll have to delay our meeting with Jean this afternoon, depending on how this turns out. Hope he left a note or some last words. Without that, we could find ourselves caught up in a more involved investigation. … Jesus, this is becoming bigger than Ben Hur!'

At the Four Wantz roundabout, Graham took the turn off to Fyfield. He hated suicides. Too much family emotion and recriminations. At least it may bring some incident to a conclusion. But it all ended up in the graveyard. Anyway, let's find out he thought.

Then he slowly put two and two together and realised. 'Hang on, Christ Ken, this is Carol Mitchell's father. This has every likelihood of being tied up with the Mia Hurley murder. I definitely do need to meet Jean, what's her name, this afternoon. Think I'm going to need the background information that she may have. Let's see what we have here first. The farm is just up this lane.'

Graham and Ken pulled up outside of the farmhouse and stepped out of the car. The Ambulance must still be on its way. That's good, thought Graham. At least the body has probably not been touched. There was another car in the drive and what looked like a wife, or now a widow, standing together. Graham walked slowly towards them.

'Hello, I'm Sgt Graham Williams from Epping Police. Are you Mrs Spicer?'

'Yes, and this is my son Glen.'

'This is Snr Constable Ken White. We are sorry for your loss and extend our condolences Mrs. Spicer. We would like to see Mr. Spicer's body if we may. I assume nobody has touched Mr Spicer?'

Glen stepped forward, 'That's correct, officer. There is also a letter from my Father in the house, but we haven't read it or opened the envelope.'

'Thank you, Mr. Spicer. We can collect it later. We will take it with us to check on any fingerprints. The ambulance will be here soon so we would like to see the body now, please.'

Glen led the way to the feed shed with Graham and Ken following behind.

Graham and Ken walked slowly into the feeding sheds. In the half-light, they could see Archer Spicer's body.

Certainly not a pleasant sight, but after a few years in policing, it becomes a bit easier to take, although a shotgun through the heart is still not a pleasant sight. Ken picked up the gun and placed it into the evidence bag.

'Well, hello, gentlemen, what do we have here?' The voice of the local pathologist coming from the doorway. 'What's happened here?'

'Suicide. There's a note left inside the house but we haven't retrieved it as yet. This may be related to a cold case that we have at Epping. See what you think. An ambulance is on its way.'

'OK. Let's have a look.'

'Ken, we need to see the letter. I'll get Glen to take me into the house so I can retrieve it. I'd like to have it analysed for prints. We also need to meet with this Jean lady in High Ongar. Stay with the Doc, I'll be back.'

Graham returned a short while later with the letter and some clothing items from Archer Spicer's cupboard.

'Just for analysis, OK Ken, let's head to High Ongar for this meeting with Jean and see what she has got to add to this whole sorry saga. May be interesting.'

Meeting with Jean.

Graham and Ken parked outside the pub and walked into the Saloon Bar. Jean was sitting there, as she said, in her red jacket' enjoying a wine.

'Hello, Jean, Sgt. Williams, and Snr Constable Ken White. How are you? Hope we haven't kept you waiting too long, we had some other matters to attend to in Fyfield.'

'No, that's fine. I always need to squeeze in some thinking time, and as I may have intimated on the phone, that time can sometimes be precious.'

'You said that you have information regarding the need to reopen the Mia Hurley case. Is that right?'

'Yes. I have connections with several people who may be involved with the Mia Hurley cold case. I was going to ask you if the information that I have will help you?'

'I see Jean. Look, in many cases, they are technically never closed, they just go cold. Some may go cold within 48 hours if all the available clues disappear. IE rain may wash away footprints.

However, we will always consider any new leads or information.

Are you able to discuss the information that you have? '

'I am, but I need to remain anonymous. These people are clients of mine. I am their Chatter and they have confided some information to me. But Mia's death happened long before I came into contact with them.'

'Perhaps if you gave me some details I may be able to see how this may impact on the Mia Case.'

'Very well. I am aware that you have been involved with the death of George Mitchell. He was married to Carol Spicer. Well, Carol has a brother, Glen Spicer, who had left Fyfield and joined the Army just before Mia's body was found.'

'Jean. At the moment we have been given some information along a line of questioning. We are currently following this up so it may be best if we contact you again as soon as we have satisfied ourselves with the relevance or otherwise. We will get back to you soon. Thank you.'

Graham turned and left the pub, and Ken followed.

Graham turned to Ken. 'A bit of a waste of time, but you never know what may come out of it. Just keep a note for a follow-up later. Let's get back to the station to see the last words of

Archer Spicer. We can have the letter tested for fingerprints.'

Chapter 22
Lizzie Hurley

Lizzie Reaches Out

Jean finished her wine and left The Foresters to head home.

Her mobile rang, and Jean answered, knowing it was Lizzie. 'Hi, Lizzie. What's up? I'm just on my way home. Just finished a meeting with Police from Epping Station. Not a lot of help but I gave them the heads up that I may have some information to help. So I'll wait and see. I let them know that I knew Glen Spicer.

Oddly enough, they mentioned that they had some information that they were following up on. No mention of what it was, but I'll dig around to see if I can find out.'

'I was just wanting to see if you know any more about Glen. I have a gut feeling that he has his fingers in this pie somehow.'

'I'll call in on Carol again. It's strange visiting her because Glen suddenly appears from nowhere. I think he stays with her sometimes. Anyway, leave it with me, and I'll get back to you.'

Jean continued on home, wondering if now was the time to look at the bank Account balance of the Orphanage.

Lizzie Calls the Police

Lizzie put her phone down and sat back in her chair. She realised that her life seemed to have been spent trying to find Mia's killer. There was an odd feeling of resentment, but she didn't know why or who it was towards.

The thought that her little sister had been raped and murdered and left lying in the mud beside the river had haunted her for years. The saving grace was that at least Mia had been treated as a cold case as opposed to being closed. But no information had been forthcoming and no further forensic evidence either seemed strange. Maybe asking Jean to help had just reinforced the fact that there was nothing more. Jean hadn't been able to produce any evidence.

Lizzie wondered if a meeting with Graham Williams at Epping police station may just bring everything to a close and she could finally give up and move on. He is always helpful and honest with me, she thought.

Just then, Lizzie's phone rang. It was the Epping Police.

'Hello, this is Lizbeth Hurley.'

'Hello Lizbeth, this is Sgt Graham Williams from Epping Police.'

'Sgt, I was just about to call you. I was wondering if you have any information. I'm feeling that I just can't go on anymore.'

'Well, that is why I have rung Ms Hurley. We have come into possession of some information that we would like to discuss with you. Are you able to call in at the Station? We can discuss the information and go over it with you.'

'I'll be there in about 25 minutes. Thank you.'

Graham turned to Ken.

'She'll be here in about 25 minutes. That poor woman has almost spent most of her life hoping to get closure on Mia's death. She's a lovely lady too. It must have been hard, but hopefully, we can finally help her now when we show her the letter from Archer Spicer.'

As she drove over to Epping, Lizzie didn't know what to feel. Would this just be another dead end that the police wanted to close, or were they going to finally close that case? That would well and truly be the end of Mia. Anyway, she drove to Epping Police Station with an open mind.

Sgt Graham Williams Delivers the News

Sgt. Graham Williams met her at the front desk.

'Thanks for coming in, Lizbeth. We know this whole episode must have taken an immense emotional toll.'

'It certainly has, but more so, the dead ends hurt. It's hard to hope for closure then be told that there is no answer.'

'Well, what we want to discuss with you may finally bring closure for you and put Mia to rest. Following a recent suicide, we received some information that we are satisfied is a conclusion to this case.

The suicide was of Archer Spicer, who, as you know, is Glen Spicer's father. Thankfully he left a letter of confession regarding raping and killing Mia. Following further discussions and investigations, DNA matches, and interviews with Glen, we are satisfied that the letter is genuine and, as far as we are concerned, brings Mia's case to an end. We can confirm that the full information is here. It was Archer Spicer who murdered Mia and not Glen, as many had believed.

If you would like to read the letter I have it on the file?'

'I feel as if I must, just to see it and be a part of it.' Lizzie picked up the letter and read it through with tear-stained eyes.

Tears flowed from Lizzie's eyes as she sat at the interview table. She stood up and walked to Graham, throwing her arms around him in a hug. Her tears flowed onto his shirt as Graham held her closely, too.

'Lizbeth, do you have anyone who can be with you at this time?' Parents or friends?'

'Not really. Our parents died some years ago. I have a couple of friends who will be happy to hear the news. Can I just stay here with you for a while?'

'Of course. Let me just get you a glass of water, and we can discuss the next steps that you may wish to take. Maybe a small celebration is called for in memory of Mia.'

'Graham, thank you so much for your support. It has been a wonderful help. I don't quite know where to go from here, but I suppose a restart of my life is called for?'

'Well, I can probably give you some tips and advice later. I have had personal experience with the sadness that you are experiencing right now. I can share some advice that I have given to other families who have lost their loved ones.'

'Thank you, that will be nice. I'll call you to make a time.' Lizzie left the Police station feeling somewhat elated. He seems a really nice man. Maybe I should take him up on his offer. So what shall I do now?

Lizzie reached her car. She picked up her phone and messaged Jean. '*Hi. Well, that's the end. Met with Sgt Graham Williams. Mia's killer was found, and it was not Glen. I am so happy. Talk soon.*

Chapter 23
Glen's Story

The Guilt

Guilt says that I made a mistake, it is shame that says I am the mistake, and that is not where I want to be.

Glen sat in his back garden, taking in the start of another day. He was used to being up at dawn.

He wondered why he was feeling so different. Why? It felt like a weight had been lifted from his chest, he could feel his breaths coming more gently.

But he couldn't stop thinking about his Mum. He would have to go and revisit her soon.

Her life had been turned upside down. In her twilight years, she had found peace now that Archer Spicer was no longer there to annoy her or remind her constantly of the contempt in which she held him.

Glen began to reflect on his own life. The way he had grown up, how he fitted into the Army. It had been an interesting experience, one that would stand him in good stead. He knew that the time would come when he had to see how he would fit into a community, what he would do with his future and, importantly, how he would have to help Carol. He wanted to ensure that she was going to be cleared of any implication in George's death. That will come, he thought.

But now, a visit to his Mum was his goal for today. He picked up his phone and called her. He waited for a few rings. A cold shiver ran through him as his intuition clicked in. His Mum had never really been on her own. Had she had a fall, perhaps? He ran to his car and drove to Fyfield as quickly as he could. Pulling up outside of the house, he ran and knocked on the front door, calling her at the same time.

'Mum, it's Glen. Are you OK?' No response. He ran to the back door, which he knew was sometimes left unlocked. He ran into the kitchen, 'Mum it's Glen, where are you? Mum, it's me.' He ran upstairs.

'Mum, it's Glen, are you OK?' With his intuition hard at work, he walked slowly into her bedroom.

It was too late. He looked at her, lying peacefully at rest. Sitting on the edge of her bed he reached and took her hand in his.

'Oh Mum, I think you just waited to see Archer Spicer punished for his sins. For what he did to all of us. I will love you always. Rest in Peace, my Dear Mum. You were not guilty of anything and you cared for us to the end. Bless you.'

With tears running down his cheeks, he walked downstairs and called the ambulance.

He sat in Mum's special chair and called Carol. He would have to be with her when he gave her the news.

'Hi, I'm coming over your way today. Will you be at home this morning? Good, I'll see you soon.

Glen knew that they would both feel guilty about what had happened in their life to themselves and Mum. They did nothing to stop it, but they were too young. Archer Spicer was a wicked man with his beatings and unkindness towards Mum. Glen would ensure that they did not carry the guilt for too long.

His Mum had finally died without him ever really developing a close relationship with her. Kept apart by the man he called Father. And then he found himself separated from his sister just so that he could escape any future beatings and not be dragged into a police matter, all because Archer Spicer had raped and killed a 14-year-old girl.

Despite feeling that a weight had been lifted from his chest there was a feeling in his heart of guilt. When he woke in the morning, he felt guilty for not doing something to save Mum or his sister Carol. He felt guilty because he had wanted to kill Archer Spicer but didn't.

As he pondered on his life's foibles, Glen realised that guilt on its own cannot solve the feelings of failure or inadequacy that he may feel. Guilt to him seems to serve as a reminder of errors or paths that should not have been taken but often were. Guilt is an opportunity to repair those errors. A chance to transform the journey to better mental stability.

Guilt serves as a warning to make amends because if you don't then you will never put things right., meaning they stay unresolved.

Glen cast his mind's eye over his past. He realised that although there may not be much that was left in his life, to put it right, there was Carol. He knew that he needed to build a closer relationship, a good old brother-sister relationship. They were growing older, time was slipping away.

He wondered idly how he could do that. Then he realised, Of Course......That's it, her children. He would help her find her children.

Seeking Children

Glen decided that he wouldn't tell Carol of his plans. He needed to have everything set up first, then tell her. After all these years, she may not want to stir that emotional pot, but there again, maybe. What about her children or grandchildren, would they want to find her, and how do they feel about not seeing their Mum for so many years?

Glen realised that he had a few problems with this idea. He didn't know their first names. At least they were boys, so they would be Spicers. One good thing was that he at least knew how to use the internet and social media. Those skills were developed when he was with Dark Justice.

With a feeling of elation, he got up and went to his computer to set up his planning. He listed the sites that he needed to visit, plus he could contact his old mates from Dark Justice. And so it began. As soon as the strategy was in place he would approach Carol with his plans.

Jean Calls

At her kitchen table, Jean sat down to review how things were going with her clients. But first, she would have a cuppa and glance through the morning paper.

What in the hell is this she said out loud to herself as she looked at the front page.

'The Essex Police have today announced that following the recent suicide of Archer Spicer, the case of the murder of Mia Hurley will be closed. Police thanked the members of the public and the Hurley family for their help.'

No, no, no, this can't be so, called out Jean. She scanned the article, but there was nothing specific. Why have they closed the case, have they arrested Glen? I'll call him to see.

Glen's phone rang. He looked at the caller ID and smiled. She didn't take long, he thought.

'Hi, it's Glen.' He answered curtly.

'Hi Glen, it's Jean. Just wondering if you are available sometime. Just wanted to have a chat. When are you free?'

'I'm free right now, deep in thought and planning though. Come on over, you have my address. See you soon.' Glen hung up.

He smiled to himself, wondering if this meeting was all about resolution, an offer to make amends and repair any damage she may have caused. Let's wait and see.

This would also be a good opportunity to talk about the orphanage that Carol was supporting. Part of his plans with Carol would be a holiday and a visit to the orphanage.

Jean Arrives

On her way over, she tried to understand what may have happened with the Police investigation. They didn't get back to her.

She arrived about 20 minutes later, having decided that she needed to sort out what Lizzie's text message was all about. She didn't want to contact Sgt Williams or Lizzie, for that matter. She felt uncomfortable about the contents of the message from Lizzie, especially as she had specifically said it wasn't Glen in her text, but heck, she was the one who thought it was Glen. She had been almost insistent that it was Glen. Had Lizzie just used her to 'stir the pot?

Oh well, the only approach was to come straight out with it. *Tell me what happened, please.*

She was feeling annoyed when she knocked on the door. Glen opened the door and smiled. 'Come on in. Tea or coffee?'

'Tea, black, no sugar, thanks.' Glen walked into his neatly set-up kitchen. 'So what can I do to help?'

'Glen, I'm confused. Lizzie sent me a message saying, *'Mia's killer found, not Glen.'* Yet when she first asked me to investigate Mia's case, she seemed convinced that you were guilty of Mia's murder.'

'Well, she thought wrong then. It was my Father. I don't need to give you any more information. It's over. No doubt there may be further info from the police about the case, but maybe not.'

'I've read the press release, but it says nothing. So who killed Mia?'

'As I said, it was my Father. He wrote the suicide note.'

'Well, I apologise if I was guilty of giving you any idea that I thought it was you. I needed to get your background facts first, which was why I ……. Oh well, it doesn't matter now.'

'That's OK. Your apology is accepted. But ……. There is something that I would like to ask you about on a totally different matter.

Now that the Mia issue is all over I want to rebuild my relationship with Carol. We spent so much time apart that I want to get to know her better.

I want to take her on a holiday, and I thought that a great place to go would be to the orphanage she supports through you. I can't find the location on the website. Can you help me, perhaps by sending me a link?'

Jean had not seen this coming. She was totally unprepared for the question. The colours in her head turned to red as the blood in her eyes throbbed. Her heart was about to stop beating.

'Of course, I can send a link. When do you plan to go?'

'Probably in about 3 -4 months. I've got to get the documents all sorted. Not sure that Carol even has a passport. So, no rush at this point.'

'That's fine. I could arrange for someone to meet you and show you around. Hope it all goes well. She needs a good restart in her life.'

Jean reached out to shake Glen's hand and turned towards the front door. She needed to get out of the house and quickly.

Glen stood and watched her walk away. Well, that was a strange reaction from her, he thought. She looked quite shocked. Hell, it was only about a visit. Thinking no further he closed the door and went back to his planning. This project had to work out well he felt.

Jean walked down the path and climbed into her car. She needed to get away as quickly as possible. She drove past The Foresters Arms and fancied calling in for a double scotch, but it was closed. Too early, damn. She needed to steady her nerves. Just get home, just get home, she muttered to herself. As she pulled into the drive, she left the car and ran upstairs to her bedroom, throwing herself on the bed.....

Angela, I need you, picking up her phone, she called Angela, but it went to message bank. . .. She spoke slowly.....'Sorry, only me. Missing you. Call when you can.'

She hung up. Christ, what will I do now, she wondered. Maybe this is it. Is this the time to take the money out of the

Orphanage Bank Account and run? There must be a fair bit in there by now. She had been doing this for quite a few years, along with the regular monthly contributions from her friends and clients plus the lump sum contributions from kind supporters.

She realised that if she is caught, it could mean prison time. This had been a good scam, but she knew the risks from the start.

Chapter 24
Glen's Goals

Carol

Glen printed out his strategy to find Carol's children. He cast a critical eye over the page. There was going to be a lot to do, and consequently, he may find himself bogged down with the details. This could be scrolling through the pages of births, deaths, marriages, electoral rolls, etc. Hell, that sounded boring. Was it all going to be worth it?

Perhaps it may be better to just find a firm that does this full-time, once Carol has given him more details. Pay a fee. Glen thought a bit further. That's it really, go to the orphanage, spend some time in Cambodia or wherever the orphanage happens to be based. He was looking at the website. Hold on, though, why isn't the location on the website? There's no 'Contact Us' tab, no phone number, or even an email address. This doesn't seem right. Maybe a chat with Joan is needed. But first of all, I'll have a chat with Carol, lay the idea on the table, and see how she feels.

Glen picked up his mobile and called Carol. 'Hi, it's Glen. I want to have a chat. When's a good time? Shall I come over now?

OK, be there soon.'

Glen pulled up at Carol's house. Epping Green wasn't that far from his place. So here goes, he thought. Step one is rebuilding.

'Hi, give me a hug. Good to see you again. Is the kettle on? I'm ready for a coffee, and I've something to talk about with you.'

Carol went into the kitchen to make the coffee. She knew how Glen liked it.

'Here you are, coffee your way. What did you want to talk about?'

Glen sat down with Carol and laid out his plan, covering the idea of looking for the children and possibly their offspring, plus a visit to the orphanage. The look on Carol's face seemed to be one of surprise, and dare he feel it, but happiness. Had he opened up a repressed memory?

'Glen, why?' Carol asked softly.

'Well, you and I didn't ever really get to know each other. You were barely 14 when I left to join the Army. Life at home was horrible for me.

Carol sat back in her chair, looking at Glen, her eyes watering. 'You do care, don't you I thought you didn't want to be my brother, that we were just part of the hell that we had been born into, part of the twisted life we had to live.'

Sometimes, I can smell his breath on me. I remember his hands feeling for me as he grunted. I wanted to kill him but was too afraid to try.

It was Mia who saved me. She would talk to me, and I remember one day he found us down by the bridge. We were talking about what was happening, but he turned up and told me to go home. I never saw Mia again. She didn't come to school anymore, and when the police came to our house, he told them that he sent Mia home. But I know he didn't I hated him, Glen. Just like I hated George for what he did to me.'

Glen wanted to tell her the truth about George but he thought better of it. He would tell her another day.

'Carol, you and I have a lot to let go in our life. We can start again, but let me be the brother that I should have been.'

He stepped towards Carol to give her a reassuring hug. In that moment, he felt the blade pierce his rib cage and enter his heart. He reached for the blade but sank to his knees and fell to the floor.

Carol picked up her phone. 'Jean, I've done what you told me to do. He is on the floor, dead!'

'What are you talking about? Who is dead?'

'Glen, you told me to kill Glen.'

'No, no, I simply said we would be better off if he was dead. I didn't mean that you had to kill him. Oh god. Okay, stay there I'm coming over. Remain calm. You just misunderstood what

I said. He would have destroyed everything we have worked for.'

'Come soon'. Carol hung up and sat on the couch, waiting for Jean. Glen would have destroyed us, she thought to herself,

Jean told me. Glen left me at the house. Men are all the same, George was horrible too. I was too young to have sex with my father. He used to hurt me, why did he do that to me? Glen would have destroyed us. Jean said so.

Slowly, the tears came to her eyes. She was thinking about the sadness of her life. The pointless years wasted on George.

Carol wanted to scream, but the emptiness in her heart gave no life. Where is Jean? I want her now. Her morbid loneliness washed over her like a wave, but the thought of making a relationship with Jean seemed to bring some feelings of pleasure.

Is that Jean pulling up now? There was a gentle knock on the front door. Carol skipped across the room to go and greet Jean.

'Hello, hello. I am so glad you are here. This way. There, he is.' Jean looked down on the body of Glen Spicer (dec'd.)

'Carol, what's done is done, but we first need to dispose of the body. You do realise that although he is dead, it will be a long time before anyone discovers he is missing. His parents are dead, he doesn't really have any friends in the area, and you are his only relative, so there is no reason to report him missing, you are not his keeper. If I am ever asked, then all I will say is that he had planned to visit the orphanage and we haven't heard from him since. It will be a long time before anyone asks.'

Carol sat and listened to Jean. She seems to understand everything.

'You can drive his car. Park at his house in the drive. We will then take the body out to Canewdon so we can sink him in the river. Strip his clothes off so that the water makes him decompose quickly. Wrap him in a blanket now and put him in the boot of my car. We will go once it gets dark. Let's have a coffee. I haven't done this before, but it was necessary for both of our sakes.'

Carol made two coffees, and she and Jean sat quietly sipping. My world is slowly changing, Jean thought, breathing a sigh of relief. At least there will be no prying eyes on the orphanage website.

Dark Justice

Meanwhile, in York, a previous work colleague of Glens, Adam (last name withheld for privacy reasons), had been working on the website that Glen had sent him earlier.

Glen had asked Adam to use his previous IT/media skills to unearth the background of the orphanage website. Glen requested Adam to decipher the coding, HTML files, the domain name registrar, the URL, and whatever else he thought necessary.

As soon as Adam had the background to the site he had planned a trip down to Epping to catch up with Glen. It had been a while since they had seen each other.

Adam set to work. The interesting thing that he found about this website, though is that it is more than likely a fraudulent website. There is no site- seal, and the TSL / SSL Certificates are missing. Adam suspects that this website is fake and used for phishing. So, where are the bank account details attached? How does money get to the orphanage? There are missing security items. This is bad news for people searching the site. Adam felt that he needed to speak to Glen rather urgently. He picked up his mobile and called Glen. The call went to message bank.

'Hi Glen, it's Adam, would you please return my call ASAP. Ta.'

Adam began to think that it was rather odd for Glen to take so long to get back to him. He rang again. 'Glen - it is Adam – I need to tell you about some issues with the orphanage website, It seems odd to me, it's probably a fake website – we need to talk about this – get back to me, please. Ta.'

Glen's Body.

As darkness fell, Jean and Carol began their body removal activity. Jean made sure that Carol drove Glen's car thereby leaving her fingerprints all over the inside. Carol drove to the house and parked in the driveway. She dropped the keys on the floor and climbed into Jean's car when she pulled up.

They headed out to Canewdon.

Being a local person, Jean knew about the darker side of the area. Canewdon is steeped in witchcraft. It is a lonely area with mud flats that fill as the tides ebb and flow on the River Crouch and its tributaries. Jean felt that this would be a good area to sink Glen's body. The river will make sure that the mud will cover the body. Afterall … it is not an area that attracts weekend walkers or hikers – perfect for hiding a body.

Jean drove into the village and went past the Anchor Public House. She knew where to go to get down by the mudflats but stopped down the road. She planned to go and have a drink in the public bar. If they were ever questioned about their activities, the visit to the pub can be a reason for being there.

Jean was making sure that she set a few obvious reasons for leaving Carol's house. She thought to herself that she could never be too sure,

Chapter 25

Adam of Dark Justice

Seeking Glen

Adam was getting frustrated. He had called Glen several times, but there were still no replies. His intuition made him suspect that something was wrong. Not only was Glen not returning his phone calls, but was not answering the emails either.

Right, he thought, I'm on my way to his place. With the determination of his investigators mind he threw some clothes and other stuff into his bag and headed to the car. He decided to drive down as he knew he would need transport once he was there.

He would send one last text message. 'Hi, on my way. There is something amiss about no replies from you. I am driving so I will be about 4.5 hours from now. CU soon.'

Adam set off, determined to find out what Glen was doing. Adam could never know what was awaiting him at Glen's house. With his foot on the pedal, he headed off to Epping.

It had been a long drive for Adam but he finally pulled up outside of Glen's house. Seeing the car in the driveway, he could only surmise that it had to be Glens, so his old friend was at home.

Well, at least he is at home, he muttered to himself. Now let's start with a cuppa and we can talk websites. He opened his car door and stepped out for a stretch. He was expecting Glen to appear in the driveway, but there was no sign. His gut instinct told him that something was wrong.

Walking over to the car, he peered inside. He knew not to touch anything until Glen appeared or at least called out to him, but silence reigned. Adam noticed the keys on the floor. Odd, he thought. That is not what Glen would do. He decided to take a walk around the house, have a look, and at least call out to Glen.

Adam wandered around to the back, calling out, ' Glen, are you here, are you here?' No responses. Perhaps another phone call may help. He dialled as he walked, and as he neared the drive, he heard the mobile ringing. It was in the car.

Adam stopped and looked around. What's happened? he wondered. Maybe I'll call in at the village pub, ask a question or two, and see if anyone has seen him recently. Adam drove down to The White Hart and pulled up on the road. He wandered up to the bar.

He approached the barman, 'Excuse me, I'm looking for a friend of mine who lives near here. Glen Spicer. Do you know him at all? It seems strange. His car is in his drive, but no sign of him.

Don't suppose you have seen him recently?'

The barman looked puzzled. 'Funny you ask that. He normally pops in for lunch and a beer but I haven't seen him for a few days. Not like him. He normally lets us know if he is going to be away. Sorry, but can't help any further.' Adam said thanks and left. He sat in his car for a few moments, thinking.

A few days, the barman said, that would be about right. He'd been calling for the last few days. Maybe ……, maybe a visit to the local police station. He checked his phone. Epping Police Station was nearest. He set off. Half-hour drive. Not far.

Adam had his story straight in his mind. He would only talk of the missing Glen. No need to mention the website issue. Keep it simple. Calling for about 3 days, car in the driveway. Keys and phone in the car, no sign of Glen. Over to them.

He pulled up outside the police station and approached the front counter.

'Hello, a friend of mine seems to be missing. He lives in Little Waltham. His car is in the driveway with the keys on the driver's side floor, and the mobile phone is inside. Not like him. I was wondering if there had been any missing person reports or should I be the first?

Adam paused, waiting to see the reaction of the front desk

officer.

'Have you made any local enquiries sir, neighbours or local shops?'

'Yes, the best place of all, the local pub, The White Hart.

He normally tells them if he is going away, but he hasn't this time.'

'Can you give me his name, sir?'

'Yes, I'm Adam, and he's Glen Spicer, and he lives in Little Waltham.'

'Right sir, if you could take a seat we'll start on the paperwork. I just have to make a call.'

The desk constable rang upstairs. 'Sgt Williams. It's Constable Richards at the front desk. Have a man who wants to report his missing friend. The missing person is Glen Spicer from Little Witham. How would you like me to handle this?'

'Thanks Constable Richards. Just start the paperwork, and I'll come down.'

Graham waited a few minutes, then wandered downstairs to the front desk.

'Hello, Adam. I'm Sgt Williams. I wonder if I may have a word with you about your friend Glen Spicer? You think he is missing?'

'Yes, I do. I have been calling him for 3 days, plus I have sent emails that he has not answered. I've known him for 9 years, and this is just not like him. Frankly, I am concerned.'

'Quite right Adam. Can I ask a few questions about Glen to help me sort this out? First, does he have any siblings or parents?'

'I know his parents have died, and he has a sister called Carol. I don't know her surname as she got married.'

'I see you live in York. Is this a social or a business visit?'

'It's really a bit of both. I've been doing a bit of research on a website he sent me. I needed to catch up with him to go over my findings as I believe it is a fake site. We used to work together.'

'And the site would be for what, sir?'

'It's an overseas orphanage that attracts donations. From my analysis a fake site like this is probably a scam.'

'Thank you for your help. Constable Richards will complete the Missing Person Report, and we will begin to make enquiries. Are you happy if we make contact with you by mobile?'

'That's fine. I'll stay in Epping somewhere, pub probably. If I can help, please just call.'

Graham stood up and took Adam to the front door. Thanking him, Graham turned and went upstairs.

'Ken. Get your coat. I'll get forensics to meet us at Glen Spicer's place. I think we have a bit of a turn-up for the books. Glen Spicer seems to be missing. Let's go and have a look.'

Meeting at Glen's place in Little Waltham, Sgt Williams spoke to Jack from Forensics.

'Jack, I'm looking for any prints inside and outside of the car. Check the keys that are on the floor and the mobile.'

Graham turned and looked around. He muttered to himself…. Well, well, what has happened here? Who has been driving in his car, and why?

'Ken, when we finish up here, we need to head over to Carol Mitchell's place. Let's see if she knows where Glen may be.'

Chapter 26
Angela's Story

A New Job

Angela took the news well. Besides, there was not a lot she could do about it.

UK universities decided to decrease the number of staff despite some of the associate professors and lecturers successfully bringing in fees. Angela was always aware of the possible changes, especially with the added decline in the number of international students. Over 50 UK Universities were in turmoil. She had to smile.

A number of her research papers (peer-reviewed) into Families and breakdowns have been published in several international journals and social media magazines. She had also been asked to submit a TED Talk application. The net result of all of this exposure was that several international universities and magazines wanted to meet her and discuss a position as a person of importance with an opportunity to be employed by them.

The disruption in her university was going to lead to more job opportunities for overseas work.

She wondered to herself, would Jean come with me? She decided that she had to meet with her and talk it through. Here was a chance to develop their relationship and travel overseas. How would she feel? I just hope she would consider coming with me.

She Called Jean

'Hello my Dear, how are you? Feeling well, I hope. Listen, I need to talk to you as soon as possible. Have some interesting news to share. Can I call over?'

'Of course. Come now. Can you stay a while, the night perhaps? I am missing being with you.'

'On my way.' Angela felt a tinge of excitement.

She pulled up at Jean's house, feeling excited about both staying the night and sharing the news.

Jean looked at Angela as she opened the door. 'OK. I can see you are excited. Is it me or the news?'

'Both. It's you and me and the news. How would you like to live overseas with me?'

Jean's mind went into a spin. This was almost too good to be true. A chance to get away from the UK, be with Angela, take the money from the orphanage account, and probably be out of reach from any possible police enquiries about Glen.

'When do we go and where are we going? This is amazing news. Can't think of anything more exciting right now. Tell me more.'

Sitting down with Jean, Angela slowly explained what had happened at the Uni and how her research had led to job offers. She had received offers from a number of Universities and magazines in Europe, the USA, and Canada. Everything seemed to have fallen into place for both of them. Only Angela was not to know just how much this was great news for Jean.

'Angela, I can promise you this. I am ready to go with you as soon as you like. I could think of nothing more wonderful. We can be together forever.' Jean let go of a small laugh. 'I'll start packing now! Let's go to bed to celebrate.'

Their passion for each other ran deep. Angela frequently gave way to loud gasps of ecstasy as Jean made sure that she would never forget just how much she needed her, just how much she wanted her, and so much more.

Angela left after breakfast. Jean sat at her kitchen table and began to reminisce about the journey that her life had taken. There was no doubt that Carol had well and truly screwed up with the killing of Glen. How could she have been so damn stupid?

Jean determined that she was not going to be caught up and dragged into this issue. If the police put that and the orphanage scam on her, then she can kiss away the rest of her life.

Angela was going to be her saviour. Move out of the UK and hide overseas. It couldn't be safer or quicker. She also realised that the time was now to draw out most of the funds in the Orphanage account, but maybe leave the account open with a small balance so the account doesn't show up as 'Closed.' Where will the money go was the next question. Her passport was in order, and she'll wait for Angela to let her know about visas. She could be a partner. Perhaps they should become engaged?

Jean soon realised that the primary object was to remain untraceable. Wow, a bit of planning is required, but everything will work out in the end, she thought.

Chapter 27

Sgt Graham Williams Snr. Const. Ken White

Glen Spicer

'Ken, I've got the fingerprint report from Jack in Forensics. I'll give you two guesses as to who they belong to.' Ken looked pensive. 'I guess female, family member, then it's his sister Carol. '

'Spot on. Grab your coat. We have an interview to conduct with one Mrs Carol Mitchell. We need to know why her prints are all over the inside of Glen's car and where the hell he is?

This is going to be quite interesting. Hang in and watch a master at work.'

They set off for Epping Green and Mrs Carol Mitchell. Graham felt his car almost knew the way to Carol's house. He sensed that there would be a few more regular visits.

They pulled up at Epping Green, parked in the drive, and walked up to the front door. A discreet knock was answered by Carol's voice calling out, 'Coming.' She opened the door, undoubtedly thinking it may have been Jean, so the surprised look on her face was noticeable to Graham.

'Mrs Mitchell, sorry to call like this, but we were just passing and wondered if you could help. May we come in?'

'Of course, come in. Take a seat. How can I help?' asked Carol, trying to stay calm but feeling absolutely shocked. Why are they here, she wondered? She was soon to find out and be shocked even further.

'We are making some enquiries regarding your brother Glen. We have received a missing person report, and as he is your brother, we were wondering if you could help. Do you know where he has gone? Is he travelling somewhere, when did you see him last?'

Graham was throwing the questions at her to put her under a bit of pressure. 'We are on our way to his house, so we thought that you might have some knowledge of his movements.'

The colour drained from Carol's face. She searched for some words. In a somewhat nervous voice, she simply said, 'Sorry, but I am not sure. Haven't seen him for a while.'

'The friend who put in the MPR said that the car was in the drive with the keys on the floor. Would you not think that leaving keys on the floor is a rather odd thing to do?

Carol just sat and nodded gently, not daring to speak. 'When did you last see him? Would it have been 2 or 3 days ago? There may be messages on his mobile because Glen had left his phone in the car. That was unusual for Glen. We should be able to see the messages or calls once we get the phone. His friend says that he rang the morning that he was coming down. Did you speak to him?'

'Only when he rang to tell me he was coming to see me.'

'Did he come over?'

Suddenly Carol realised that she had spoken. Her head was aching. She saw images of her father questioning her, and she heard George's voice telling her how stupid she was.

'I don't remember, I don't remember.' Carol was becoming emotional. Graham stopped.

'Sorry Carol, I didn't mean to upset you. It's OK. Perhaps we should talk tomorrow. We can call around in the morning. We'll let ourselves out. See you tomorrow.' Graham and Ken stood up and headed for the door, leaving Carol in a mess.

They got into the police car and headed to Glen's house. Ken turned to Graham. 'What are your thoughts? You didn't tell her about the forensic report.'

'That is for tomorrow. Something is a little wrong here. Let's see the car again and retrieve the phone. If he did ring her, then we need to bring her in and have a thorough talk.'

When they arrived at Glen's house, they went to the car. Graham opened the door and looked in the glove box. Voila, there was the phone.

'That wasn't hard. Now let's see what the text's history and missed calls tell us.'

There was still a charge in the battery, so Graham turned the phone on and selected Calls and messages.

'Well, well, well, what have we found here? 3 days ago, a call to Carol about coming over to see her. Then, there were several missed calls from the same number, and I suspect it was Adam.

Ken, I think our friend Carol has had a bit of a memory freeze. I think we need to interview her at the Epping police station tomorrow. Let's just have a read through the phone, and we can go back to base and log this case further. I'll give her a call now and arrange to see her around 12. Let's go back to Epping now and write this up so far. I don't think she was too happy about coming in, and she didn't ask for legal support. I don't want to concern her too much right now, so I'll call her in the morning and suggest that she get legal support. I know her solicitor in town. Kelvin Hunter and Associates.

Carol to Jean

As soon as the front door closed, Carol reached for her phone and rang Jean.

'Jean, I think we are in trouble. The Epping police were here again. I have to report to Sgt Williams tomorrow at 12. Someone lodged a Missing Persons report about Glen. I thought you said that nobody would know that he is missing because he has no friends here.

They have been to his car. Oh hell, what are we going to do???? '

'Calm down, Carol. Slow down and think. What did they say?'

Jean and Carol discussed the events of the meeting with the police. She didn't mention about blurting out about Glen.

After a while, Jean began to feel as if her world was about to cave in on her. This was not a good feeling. She needed to get out of here soon. Maybe leave the UK now for a 'holiday?'

'Carol, I'll come around tomorrow morning. Stay calm and have a good night's sleep. We can work out our story then. See you tomorrow.'

Epping Police Station Graham and Ken

Sitting back in his chair, Graham turned to Ken.

'So let's have a look at where we are and what seems to be the story so far. We can get a lot of background on Glen and Carol from the investigation into the death of Mia Hurley. If we look back at their history, we can see that Glen and Carol spent their teen years growing up in Fyfield but apart. Glen is in the Army, and Carol

leaving school, doing nursing at Epping Hospital, and then marrying George.'

'So then Glen eventually returns home, and they appear to be getting together. Carol is certainly suffering from the mental abuse brought on by George. ….. But 3 days ago, Glen called wanting to come over to see Carol. It then appears that he is not seen or heard from again. That is clear from the 'missed calls and unanswered emails' that Adam had sent. What happened?'

'Next question. How did his car get back to his house? It is a fair distance from Carol's house, so there has to be another person involved. I think at some point, I will ask Carol directly as to who else was involved. That may elicit a response, confused or otherwise.'

'We should also make a call at The White Hart tomorrow morning before Carol comes in. See if they recall Glen's last visit. Oh well, that's enough for today. See you tomorrow morning about 9.'

Jean Calls Angela

'Hello, my dear lady. How are you? I have been thinking. If a new role turns up for you soon, that will be fantastic, but right now, I really feel that I need a bit of a holiday. I haven't been to the orphanage for a while, so I thought that I should pop over to

Cambodia for a visit to have a look at what they may need to do. The donations have built up, so we should invest them into something worthwhile. Maybe a new residential building or an additional classroom. Are you OK with that? '

'Of course. That sounds like a wonderful idea. You are an amazingly thoughtful person. It may take a while before I accept a post, and then I will go through the process of visas and work permits. If you are already overseas, it may be easier to travel wherever I am going. I'm going to miss you. When are you planning to leave?'

'I was thinking reasonably soon. I'm excited about the chance to travel a bit, so I'll start the process and then give you a call when the dates are organised. I'm going to miss you too, but it will only be for a short while. Let's get together for a goodbye fling before I leave.'

Angela agreed to the idea of Jean taking a holiday, knowing that she would miss their intimate moments, however, plans must be plans, so it shouldn't be too long before they got together again.

Jean hung up with a feeling of freedom in her heart. She thought she should take the chance to get out of the UK, leaving Carol to carry the can and go somewhere that would give her some security and obscurity and at the same withdraw the funds from the orphanage bank account.

The next thing was the bookings. She smiled to herself, 'There's no bloody orphanage in Cambodia connected with me, but I may as well go there anyway.' She picked up her mobile and connected to the trailfinders.co.uk website. Her needs were simple, a single ticket to Cambodia, landing at Phnom Penh International Airport, and finding a local motel for temporary accommodation. Trailfinders would do all that for her.

Jean thought about how her life had gone. She planned to merge into the community by dressing in traditional style and, for all intents and purposes, looking very much like a resident. She would find local accommodation away from the initial motel. If it was easier, she would take all of the funds from the Orphanage Account and keep them in local currency in her possession or a safety box somewhere.

Jean finally smiled to herself, feeling that this was her perfect disappearing trick.

Chapter 28
Lizzie's Story

A New Life

Since Lizzie's last text to Jean regarding who had killed Mia, her life has changed. No more emotional turmoil, no more internal anger, no more talking to Jean, and lots more spare time. She has been able to focus more on her business development. The 'Social Dynamics in the Workforce' business has seen an increase in the number of clients. Lizzie is rather pleased with the growth. However, the missing element in her life was the friendship of a man.

She noticed that after a long day of working, she would only sit alone in her garden with no one to talk to. She decided that this had to change. She was still a young woman with a lot to share with a man. After all, she was still in 'childbearing age.' She smiled to herself....... if there was a man seeking to have children. Being alone was one thing, but sharing some loving was a totally different option.

As she got to thinking, she remembered that after Mia's ' Life Commemoration' service, Sgt Graham Williams had spoken to her, offering to 'extend the hand of friendship.' Was that a sort of subtle way to say, 'Let's get together.' Lizzie decided that she would check out the offer. She picked up her mobile and called Sgt Graham Williams.

'Hello, Ms Hurley, nice to hear from you.'

'Call me Lizzie, please, Sgt Williams.'

'And you call me Graham.'

'Thanks, Graham. I'm not sure if you remember, but after Mia's service, you mentioned the offer of a chat. Well, if it is OK with you, I would like to take you up on that offer. Time has passed, and I think that I am ready to be myself. Ready to live a normal existence. So, is your offer still open?

'It certainly is, and I would look forward to catching up with you. So when would suit you? I have to check with my shifts.'

Lizzie liked that response. No mention of a wife or a partner. Things may look up.

'Lunch or after-work drinks? You tell me.'

'Well, I work from home in my own business, so am free at any time.'

They finally agreed to meet at the Horse and Jockey in Tylers Green the following evening. Lizzie didn't mention that she lives in Tylers Green, although she guessed that Graham would know anyway.

She wondered how things would go. She hadn't been on a 'date' for many years! She was looking forward to an exciting outcome. Maybe something with a future so that her life would turn out for the better.

Chapter 29

Sgt Graham Williams and Const. Ken White

The Interview

Graham and Ken met to go over the case notes. Their meeting at The White Hart was interesting. The barman confirmed that Glen had not been in during the previous day.

'So Glen's phone call to Carol seems to indicate that there was some personal connection between them. He must have gone to Carol's house to see her and talk, but what about?

At 12, Carol entered the Epping Police Station. She felt petrified but knew that she had to go through the interview. She felt a little better when she saw her solicitor, Kelvin Hunter, sitting and waiting for her.

No sign of Jean, though, not that she expected her to be here.

Graham let them sit and wait for a few minutes before sending Ken to take them to the interview room. After collecting the case file, Graham went to start the interview.

'Hello, Mrs Mitchell. Thank you for coming in. As you know, we are looking for your brother, Glen Archer. His disappearance was reported to us by a friend of his, and from our visit to the house and inspection of the car, it seems clear that he has certainly disappeared, so our question is where to and how?'

Carol felt a surge of anger when Graham mentioned that a friend had reported him missing. Jean had distinctly told her that nobody would know, and now she was being interviewed because a friend had reported him missing. CAROL WANTED TO SCREAM.

'Mrs Mitchell, do you know how his car got back to his house? We are aware that he rang you to arrange a time to come over and visit you. So we know that he was in your house. So, how did his car get back to his house? We would believe that there had to be another person in the house at some time……?

Carol sat in silence, not knowing what to say. Ken sat looking at her. ' Carol, did you ever drive the car?' She shook her head. 'Well, that is strange because your fingerprints are all over the inside, particularly on the driver's side.'

Graham could see that this interview would go on for a while. Perhaps he had better ask some leading questions.

'So, was Jean in your house later that day? Did she follow you back to Glen's house that night thinking that nobody would see you?'

Once again, Carol shook her head. She felt that she had to protect Jean, but she needed Jean to tell her what to say and what to do. She knew that without Jean, she could end up being charged with Glen's murder. Jean told her that the police would never know, but she also said that nobody would know Glen was missing, but they do know! They do know! Jean felt sick to her stomach.

She would call Jean as soon as the interview finished. But when would it end?

Graham looked at Carol.

'Carol, we don't believe that you were involved in Glen's disappearance on your own. Why don't you tell us who else was involved?'

'I can't. She said nobody would know.'

'Who said that? Was it your friend? If it was your friend, then that person should talk to us about what happened. We do not believe you did this on your own. Where is Glen now?'

Graham looked at Kelvin. It was evident that he was sympathetic towards Carol but surely must see the logic of the questions. There seemed to be no option than to stop the meeting now and resume again tomorrow.

Graham also had an important meeting tonight.

Graham stood up. 'We may as well stop at this point and resume again tomorrow. Carol, I would like to ask you to think carefully about what your actions have been and tell us a couple of things tomorrow. Where is Glen now? What happened to him, and who helped you? Thank you for your time, and we will meet tomorrow at 10. You may want to talk to your solicitor, too.'

Graham folded the file and walked out. He waited for Ken to get upstairs. 'I couldn't see much point in continuing. We need to let her stew a bit, so we may get a different response tomorrow. Hopefully, Kelvin will try to talk some sense into her. I have another meeting. See you tomorrow.

Graham turned and walked downstairs to head off to his meeting with Lizzie. He would get to the Horse and Jockey pub a bit before their agreed meeting time so that he could relax for a while. Ordering a half pint, he sat down at a table with a couple of chairs. No sooner had he sat down when he heard a gentle voice behind him say, 'Good evening Graham, you seem to be a bit early too…… I hope, like me, you are looking forward to our meeting.'

Graham turned to look at Lizzie. He was shocked. Wow …. This was not the lady he had met before. There was no funny hairstyle, no coloured hair strands, no black mascara, no anxious pulling of the hair, just a beautiful, happy-looking lady. Graham let out a deep breath.

'Wow, I was expecting to meet Lizzie, who are you? Without a doubt, the most alluringly beautiful lady here tonight.'

'Why thank you, sir, that is mighty kind of you to say that.' Lizzie replied with a gleaming happy smile on her face

They both laughed, the ice was broken, and the night would go well.

'Let me buy this beautiful lady her drink. What will it be? A pinot gris, I would guess?'

'My word, you are a good detective! You are right, a pinot gris it is, please.' Graham went to the bar to buy the wine for Lizzie, feeling somewhat excited. The only memory he has of Lizzie is back when the Mia case was open, but she has changed so much. He could feel a wonderful future opening up for him or for them.

'Your wine, madam.' Graham put the wine down and sat beside Lizzie.

Carol calls Jean

Carol and Kelvin left the police station together. Reaching Carol's car, Kelvin turned to her.

'Carol, if you don't open up about who was involved with you and where Glen's body is, then you are going to be in a lot of trouble. More than likely be treated as the main suspect, and this will not be good for you. I ask that you speak to whoever was involved with you, and I can arrange for the next steps. We will need a barrister if you are charged with murder.'

Carol froze at the thought. What happens if they start to investigate George's death next? She thanked Kelvin, climbed into her car, and headed home. She had to talk to Jean.

On arriving home, she knew that the first thing she needed was a cup of sweet tea. She was in shock. She sat down to try and 'get her head straight.'

Picking up her mobile, she rang Jean. After a few rings, it went to message bank. 'Damn,' she cursed and left a 'call me' message.

It slowly dawned on her that she was heading into deep trouble, and she was not going to take this on her own.

Jean was involved. It was Jean who persuaded her to kill Glen. Jean had lied to her. She didn't really know that nobody would miss Glen, she didn't know that none of his friends would know, and she didn't know what would happen at all. That was why she made me drive the car, and that was why she made me go into the pub in Canewdon to buy the drinks. She was making me look guilty.

She was beginning to feel the same as she felt when George used to make her do things that she didn't want to do.

Carol closed her eyes. If Jean doesn't call me back soon, I'm going to tell Sgt Williams the truth at the meeting tomorrow. She rang Jean again, but the call went to the message bank.

Carol opened her eyes. I'm telling Sgt Williams the truth, she said out loud. She made one more call to Jean. Message bank again. She turned her phone off.

Jean had seen Carol's calls but decided not to talk to her. Any conversation was going to confuse her. Jean knew that she should be on a plane soon and getting out of the UK. Any discussions with Carol would only end up dragging her into the police enquiry, and that may stop her going.

Jean's phone rang again. Angela was calling. She let it go to message bank.

Where do they live?

Jean …Readings Farm Road, Witham

Evelyn…… Willingale Road, Norton Heath

Carol…Epping Road, Epping Green

Angela… Essex Uni, Colchester

Liz Hurley……. Weald Bridge Road, Tylers Green.

Glen Spicer… The Street, Little Waltham,

Sgt Graham Williams and Const..Ken White …. Epping Police Station

Graham Williams ……… Dukes Road, North Weald.

About The Author

Peter J Morley. A Writer of Novels, Poetry and Short Stories ….

Peter was born in February 1947. His early childhood was spent growing up in Khartoum, Sudan.

In 1954 his parents returned to England as Sudan gained independence from the British Commonwealth in January 1956. On his return to England, he was enrolled in his boarding school in Truro, Cornwall where he stayed until 1963.

Peter started writing poetry and stories in 2018 following an unusual event in his bedroom.!! As he was getting into bed a verse came into his head…… *If I could take my first breath again, And know what I would learn, I'd set myself upon a path, From which I would not turn……*

Peter got up, wrote that poem and since then has found great solace in the writing of poetry and short stories and now The Chatters Web. The short stories are often inspired by his poetry.Peter covers many social issues, moments in history humour, sadness, depression, mental health and most importantly, like many other poets, ……. Love.

Now retired Peter spends much of his time involved in community work through his local Rotary Club, as treasurer for a

Community Bank, President of Redcliffe Meals on Wheels and a District Ambassador for Shelter Box.

ShelterBox is based in Truro, Cornwall in England. This is where Peter went to school.

Peter donates a percentage of the sales of the book to ShelterBox www.shelterboxaustralia.org.au. Shelter Box is a registered charity.

Notes.